# THE CHRONICLES OF JACK MARSHALL

## MARSHALL

SEXCAPADES

C. J. SLATER

# THE CHRONICLES OF JACK MARSHALL
## SEXCAPADES

*BY*

## C.J. SLATER

ISBN: 979-8-9888371-3-8
COVER DESIGN: *WAKADA DESIGNS*
IMAGES: *ROMANCE COVER MODELS; COPYRIGHT TO MATTHEW HULL*
OTHER IMAGES: *DEPOSIT PHOTOS*

IWRITESMUT.COM

# MUSIC PLAYLIST

*Climax* by Usher

*Haunted* by Beyonce

*I Wanna Know* by Joe

*Kiss It Better* by Rihanna

*Wicked Game* by Chris Isaak

*if u think i'm pretty* by Artemas

*Lion* by Beast Inside Beats

*Rude Boy* by Rihanna

*Pillowtalk* by Zayn

*Dive* by Usher

# CONSENT

Jack Marshall always gets consent to fuck the bad girl out of his sexual partners. At the beginning of their relationship all aspects of limits, boundaries, and safe words has been discussed—mostly off page. The exception is Mel Bellamy. He didn't establish a consent conversation with her because he continuously believes he won't fuck her but then does anyway. Poor Jack is in denial. But before he has sex of any kind with her, he does the right thing and gains consent.

## XXX WARNINGS

*The Chronicles of Jack Marshall: Sexcapades* is an open door erotic romance and is meant for an adult audience. *18+ only, please.* If you have any sensitivity concerns or triggers, please read this list prior to reading the stories that follow. Your well-being is paramount. Take care of you. You matter. Even if you think you have no concerns over content, please read the list so you know what you are getting into. Not every book is meant for every reader. Make sure this one is your jam. Love you guys!

**Explicit language.** Fuck is used as a noun, a verb, an adverb, an adjective and everything in between. Some lighter usage of ass, shit, damn, dammit, and godammit. And because Helena has a foul mouth—cocksucker, motherfucker, asshole, and bastard. Jack uses degrading names with his 'friends,' such as bitch, cunt, and cum slut as part of dominance play.

**Graphic sexual scenes.** Including oral and anal sex. Jack's favorite position is doggy style and he likes anal play, a lot. He's also been known to use spit as lube. Kinky play includes restraints, butt plugs, remote control vibrators, Ben Wa balls, spanking, punishment, sex in front of others, third-party sex, rough sex, sex in public places, and sex club play.

# DISCLAIMER

Although BDSM, kinky play, and dom/sub relationships are topics included in these stories, it is all pure fantasy meant to titillate and inspire. It is not meant to replicate the dynamics of these real and complex relationships. Jack is only here for a hot and sexy escape. So, please—enjoy!

# PROLOGUE
## BELLINGHAM, WASHINGTON - SUMMER 2023

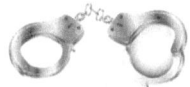

It's the perfect sunny day by the water. My large frame is leaned against my black 1969 Mustang as I people-watch. Well, in this case one person—a gorgeous brunette in tight short-shorts who's jogging up and down the boardwalk in front of me. Her hair tied into side ponytails—a little too girl-next-door for my taste. I try to ignore her, but that ass jiggling in the midday sun is almost too much to take. She glances over at me and my dick twitches. I maintain my stare causing her to blush. Despite my best intentions, I want to ruin her.

Her glossy red lips make a perfect pout as she checks her Fitbit on her fourth pass. I should leave so I don't get caught up with this little bitch. I'm not in the mood to train another sub. She bends over to tie her sneaker and all I see is her perfectly round ass. My dick twitches again. Not now. This isn't the girl for us. It's not worth it, boy. I stand up and turn towards my car.

My hand is on the door handle when I hear a woman's voice. "Hey."

Looking over my shoulder I see that it's her— pouty lip girl. She licks her lips. The sun is pretty high in the sky making her eyes squint as she looks up at me. I grunt in response as I open my door. Her arm darts out and grabs a hold of my arm, catching it by my elbow. Slow as fuck I turn around. My imposing 6'4 frame blocks out the sun. I glare at the hand that's still on my arm, then meet her gaze with a scowl.

Instantly she retracts her hand. "Shit! I'm sorry."

She started this. Now she's gonna have to tell me what she wants. She toys with one of her long silky ponytails wrapping it around her finger. She bites her bottom lip. Jeezus. She knows exactly what she's doing. Not so innocent after all. "I-I'm Kara," she stutters.

I grunt.

"Um... I couldn't help but notice... I mean, you're in a suit." She forgets herself and brushes her hand against my bulging bicep, then quickly removes it.

She glances around at the busy boardwalk. "Everyone else is in shorts." I glance down at hers—skin-tight yoga shorts that perfectly highlight her bubble butt. My eyes move up her whole body until I'm staring into her beautiful blue-green eyes, crystal-clear like Colchuck Lake. Her long dark eyelashes flutter as she works out a half-smile. "You're awfully big..."

I turn to go. This chick is wasting my time.

"Wait! Won't you tell me your name?" She pauses, then says softly, "Please?"

That last word—my heart pounds outta my chest. "Jack."

Her face and neck turn a pretty shade of pink. "Well, Jack... pleased to meet you." She reaches out to shake my hand and brushes against my abs. My whole body quivers inside. Shit. "Maybe I could get to know you better..." she offers. The lustful look in her eyes tells me she isn't talking about going for coffee.

I open my car door, motioning to her. "Get in." I hold the side of the roof and slide in. She jogs over to the passenger door, opens it, and hops in. Out of the corner of my eye I watch her hands fidget nervously on her lap. "Sure about this?" I ask.

She shakes her head yes. "I want this."

"What do you want?" My voice is low and husky.

Her eyes are downcast as she rubs her palms against her thighs. "I want... I want..."

"Tell me." I command.

She swallows hard as she looks into my eyes. "I want... you."

My mouth twists into a sinful smile. I stick my key in the ignition and turn it on, revving the engine a few times, then shift it into gear. My arm stretches across the back of her seat. Before I back out of my parking spot, I glance over at her. "Hold on. It's gonna be a hell of a ride."

# JACK MARSHALL & ROSE BUSH

## THE PUNISHMENT
### JUNE 2024

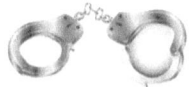

My eyes devour Rose as she stands on my doorstep. Her fitted peach-hued dress hugging every damn curve. My mouth waters seeing her big crimson colored lips and I already want to bite them. Though I haven't known her for long, what I've discovered is that underneath that sweet put together exterior is a straight freak. I've made it my mission to get to that juicy center but it takes time, intention, and patience. Luckily, I have all three. The payoff will be worth it. Because when I break her, she belongs to me.

She's already giving away how she feels. The way she's toying with her gold hoop earrings. Her eyes looking down and away. She's upset with me and conflict makes her nervous. I know why she's upset. I fucked up and I already know what I'm going to do about it. But I know Rosey, she needs a minute to get it all off her chest. She glances up and me then looks away again. For some reason, seeing her like this is a huge turn on. My dick is already getting hard.

"Jack, I waited for you," she says. I can see she wants an explanation, a reason. The truth is I got caught up with work. I was on a stake-out and forgot all about our date. But I wanna make her sweat it out so I don't say anything. "You said it was our night. I thought..." she says, eyes downcast. Her hair has fallen forward covering her pretty green eyes.

I tilt her chin up with my forefinger and thumb. She meets my gaze. "What did you think, Rosey?"

She bites her lip. "You know, Jack."

I lean against the door casing, my large muscular frame towering over her. I've got her where I want her. Her discomfort is driven up as I force her to stand outside on my doorstep. My arms are crossed at my chest. "Nah, I don't think I do." My eyes are fixed on her. "Why don't you tell me?"

She swallows hard. When she looks up at me again her eyes soften, nearly melting my resolve. But

I'm not giving in. Not yet. I need to see how far I can push her. I need to know what she'll do. She plays with her hair, twirling it around her fingers. "I wanted..."

"Tell me." My response is low and growly.

"I wanted you," she says, as her face and neck turn a pretty shade of pink.

I shift my body so my back is now against the door casing, making room for her to walk through. As she quickly brushes past me, the sweet scent of jasmine fills my inhalation. *Fuck.* She smells good. I want to wrap her into me, get her naked, make her mine. The waiting is punishment on its own. She walks through and into the hall and I close the door behind her. The way that dress hits all her curves is perfection. That ass is fucking bitable and I want to claim it. She turns around and gazes at me so innocently I almost feel bad for what I'm about to do. Almost.

I pull her into me and her tits press against my abs. My blue eyes hone in on her. "You're right. I did promise to spend the night with you." I brush the back of my hand against her cheek. "I'm sorry."

Her smile doesn't reach her eyes. "It's alright."

"No...it was rude of me." I run my nose along her

jawline. My cock twitches in my trousers. "Tell you what," my forefinger grazes her juicy bottom lip. She's hanging on my every word. "I'll let you punish me."

She gasps and her mouth makes an *o*. "I couldn't."

"I'm giving you permission, just this once. Take it," I insist.

Rose walks across the room, giving me another look at that round ass. I'm like a panther—watching, waiting, eyeing its prey. I'm genuinely curious what she'll do next. Pushing my girl's limits makes my blood rush through my veins. All I want to do is bend her over and fuck the shit out of her, take that perfect ass, but now is not the time. I've got to push aside my deviant thoughts so I'll be ready when she lets go—when she's set free.

She turns abruptly on her heel. "Alright."

I swallow hard, as I close the distance between us. "Alright what, Rosey?"

Another step forward, this one is hers. So brave, my little cum slut. "I-I'll punish you."

A wicked smile spreads across my lips. "Will you now?"

She nods.

"Let's hear it."

My little Rose stands in front of me. Her eyes are dark with desire and, if I'm not mistaken, a little power. "All in good time... mustn't rush these things."

I smirk, so proud of my girl. "Right."

She paces back and forth in front of me as she talks. "After all, knowing what I'm about to do *might* put you at ease." She stops and stares at me. "And you don't deserve that... you were very naughty."

My Adam's apple bobs in my throat as my adrenaline spikes.

"I mean, I might even enjoy giving punishments," she says breathily. "Although, not nearly as much as I like receiving them."

My eyes widen. I didn't expect that from her. I've never seen her like this. My instinct was spot on. I made the right decision pushing her. This side of her makes me as hard as a rock.

Rose gazes intently at me. With her left hand, she pulls her hair to the side, revealing her long neck. My cock twitches. "Take your clothes off."

Without a word, I take my navy suit jacket off. I rip the light blue dress shirt from my trousers, unbutton it, and take it off—my heart pounding in my chest. I drape my clothes over the bar stool next to me. Never taking my eyes off her, I unbuckle my belt, unzip my fly, and shift my trousers and boxer briefs down my legs. One leg at a time, I remove them, setting them over my shirt. My dick is standing to attention, throbbing and bobbing, like he's trying to reach Rosey. Not yet, boy. Our girl needs to punish us first.

She rubs her chest, like she's heating up inside. I don't think she realized how it would feel to punish me. The proof is in her eyes—they're dark and wild. It's making her completely feral. I knew she was a freak, but this is on another level. I'm watching her every move.

Something comes over her, a crooked grin creeps across her mouth. She leans over and grabs my pants off the chair and pulls the belt through the loops of my trousers. I wonder what she'll do with that. My dick twitches at the prospects.

"Kneel."

My 6'4 frame towers over her, yet she has me by the balls. I get down on my knees, awaiting her instructions. Rose wraps the belt around my thick neck, fastening it as tight as it will go. *Fuck.* She's using my belt as a makeshift collar. This is fucking hot. I'm the punisher. I never imagined that I'd get off on *being* punished.

"N-now, you will do as I say." Shit, I've created a

monster. "And don't make a sound." The way she's looking at me with contempt has my cock throbbing. I let out an unintentional moan. Her hand on her hip, she shoots me a look of displeasure. "You moaned."

Fuck. My pulse races. I'm dying to know what she'll do to me. "I did. What are you going to do about it?" I pant, breathless.

"I'll need to punish you," she says, reaching up and yanking on my makeshift collar and leash. "Come." The sun is low in the sky as she leads me outside. With no fence or even bushes to hide my huge naked body, anyone could see me. "Now, stand out here until I tell you. Don't move."

Jeezus. Public nudity, treating me like a dog— this is aggressive, especially for her. Rose slowly runs her fingers from my chest all the way to my groin. My dick is throbbing and bouncing for her. "Stay," she says forcefully. She turns on her heel and goes back inside. Back into the comfort of my warm house while she leaves me shivering in the cool evening air. I've never felt this turned on in my life and from punishment no less. All I can think about is what I'm going to do to her once I get my hands on her.

A string of my pre-cum hangs off the tip of my

cock, dripping down into a pool on the concrete beneath me. I'm so hot and bothered, if a breeze blows, I'll explode. I'm outside for what feels like fifteen to twenty minutes, just dripping, throbbing, and shaking. The thought that anyone could walk by and see me is driving me insane.

When Rosey finally returns, she's wearing nothing but a black see-through bra and matching panties. "Heel," is all she says when she yanks on my leash. She walks me back inside and like the horny boy that I am, I follow her willingly. She leads me through the kitchen, up the stairs, and into my bedroom, leaving me in the middle of the room. "Stay." I run my hand through my wavy, dirty-blonde locks, licking my lips, and eyeing the bed the whole time. The ache in my groin is growing by the second. Not yet. Patience.

My girl lightly runs her fingers up my thighs and over my stomach, making my whole body lurch. I'm dying. I need release. I watch as she slips her panties down her legs and steps out of them. She's so fucking hot. Her hand dips between her legs and she starts rubbing her clit, biting her lip as she does. Her other hand pops her tit out of her bra. She moans and massages it, pinching her nipple. She's pleasuring herself—right in front of me. *Fuck*. I mean, I'm disciplined but she's pushing it.

She's going to live to regret it.

I try to grab her titties and she smacks my hand away. "Don't touch."

I let out a low growl and her eyes widen. My greedy eyes watch as she spreads herself open before dipping her finger inside of her. Her tongue quickly licks her lips. "Ahh..." she moans.

F.U.C.K. That pussy looks so tight. I want my cock in her so bad. I'm imagining how it'd feel gripping my hard length. "Jeezus, Rosey... What are you doing to me?"

She moans through her response, "If-if you're good, I-I-I might get you off."

Dirty little cum slut. It takes every ounce of self-control not to fuck her right now. My eyes take in every inch of her writhing body—how her back arches, eyes half-closed as she throws her head back. She bites her lip and her body shakes as she climaxes, cursing as she does.

I'm completely feral now. "You see this, Rosey." I hold my pulsating cock in my hand. "This is what happens when you make me watch you play with your fucking little pussy," I moan.

My girl looks up at me through her eyelashes,

smirking as she sticks a finger into her wetness. When she pulls it back out it's coated in her creamy cum. She steps forward and reaches up to offer me a taste of her dripping finger. I open my mouth, craving the taste. "I wanted you to know exactly what you were missing," she moans.

I latch onto her finger and suck it, ravaging every drop of her sweet juice. Then take her finger with my teeth. This little girl better watch herself. I will end this fucking game and make her regret every last word. My dick will be shoved so far inside her that she won't be able to see straight.

I feel her warm breath on my skin. "Stay still," Rose commands.

I'm aching as she brushes a finger over the tip of my cock. My dripping wet, needy, and throbbing cock. Her finger strokes up the back of it making my body jerk uncontrollably. I'm not even breathing right now.

"Jeezus," I moan, as she rubs her wet pussy against my thigh. "Rosey, I'm gonna hold you down and fuck that pretty little throat," I threaten, clenching my fists. I'm quivering. I need to cum. *Now*.

She brushes the tips of her fingers over my abs

and down my V. "You're so naughty. Such a little deviant," she says, egging me on.

I snicker but it's more like a warning. "You have no idea."

Her hand is dangerously close to my groin. "I'll tell you what, get me off then I'll let you do whatever you want to me."

My eyebrows jump. "Really?"

She pats her pussy. "On your knees."

"Yes, ma'am," I kneel down obediently in front of her.

I give her pussy a light slap. "Ahh!" she moans.

"Mmm..." With my hand I spread her open before diving in, ravishing her sweet, tender pussy. My tongue circling her clit, teasing and sucking her.

She grabs the back of my head, fisting my hair. "Fingers inside me, now."

So bossy, but I do as she says—for now. I slip a finger in, pushing it in and out of her pussy.

"Oh yeah, like that."

I add a second finger and she moans louder. She's so wound up it won't take much. Licking and finger-fucking her sweet-ass pussy is driving me insane. My dick is dripping, leaving a puddle of pre-cum on the floor. I suck her clit and her whole body tenses.

"That's right," she cries out. "Fuck!" She grabs my hair, pulling it hard. Her body shakes and jolts as she cums all over my fingers. I keep licking like a rabid beast, lapping up every drop of her sweet cum.

Her body slumps against me. Now that my girl is fully satisfied, I stand back up, wiping my mouth on the back of my hand. I pick up her limp body and toss her onto the bed. "My turn."

# ROSE BUSH

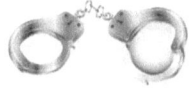

Jack's eyes are blown out and the look on his face—I think I pushed him too far. So far, he's been gentle with me, sweet even. But now I know I'm in trouble. His body is hovering over mine. He feels primal and raw. I'm both intimated and completely turned on. Out of nowhere, his arm slides underneath me and flips me over. His strong arm around my waist quickly lifts my hips into the air. I feel cool metal against my wrists and hear a click, my arms are now restrained behind my back. Without warning, he pushes inside me with his thick cock.

"Aaah!" I cry out. The feeling of fullness as he thrusts into me is intense. "Please..." I whine, unsure what I'm asking for. Unsure what I need. He's moving at a punishing pace and there's something about it that feels so animalistic. The harder he pounds into me, the more I feel—my body awakening to his touch.

"You feel so fucking good," he groans. He rubs his thumb along the crease of my ass as he thrusts. His finger circles my puckered hole a few times before slipping inside me. I feel so full—his cock filling my pussy and his large finger inside my ass. He grips my hip using it as leverage to pound me harder.

"Jack, please..."

"Relax," he groans.

I can no longer see straight. I don't know if I'm breathing anymore. Everything has gone light, my mind blank. A pleasure-filled pain has taken over every inch of my skin, my insides. I feel like I'm floating—higher and higher. All of a sudden I hit a wall, the pressure inside me, the feeling of fullness increases to an almost unbearable level, like I'm desperate to pee. I feel like I need to stop and suddenly I explode, squirting everywhere. I cum so hard that it's literally dripping down my legs.

"Oh Rosey, you're gonna make me cum. That pussy's so fucking wet," he groans still pounding into me. "Your pussy is pulling the cum out of me."

His thumb is now out and he has a hold on both hips. "Mmm... fuck yeah..."

I can't hear anything but my own screams, his moans, and the slapping of his body against my ass. "So fucking hot... look at that sweet ass." He sucks his teeth. "Shit... oh, damn..." He leans forward and wraps his hand around the front of my throat. "Such a tight little pussy." He slaps my ass, hard. "Ah fuck, I'm gonna cum." He slows down, thrusting a few more times as he finishes. "Unh..." he grunts and slumps over me. "Oh... mmm... fuck... you came all over me," he snickers.

I'm too blitzed to say anything. Too dazed to comprehend that I just squirted for the first time and it's everywhere. I feel like he fucked the life out of me. I can't think, can't speak. I'm out of my body, possibly on another planet. He lets go of my hips and my body falls to the mattress. He releases the restraints and I immediately rub my sore wrists. He really worked me over. Even my pussy is sore.

He slides his hand down my back. "You want a shower?" he says near my ear.

I nod. Still feeling unstable.

Jack flips me over gently, then offers his hand. I scoot to the edge of the bed, where he helps me up and guides me over to the bathroom. He can be so sweet and caring, especially afterwards. That's the thing that most of my friends don't understand. Yes, he's relationship-phobic and yes, he seems gruff and punishing, but there's more to him. He also happens to be a fuck of a lot of fun—if you can get past all his hang-ups. He's helped me so much. I used to be shut-down. I didn't even know how I felt or what I wanted. Now, I'm much more comfortable in my own skin. I say what I want and feel more confident, even in my regular life.

The only trouble is that I'm falling for him. It's an impossible situation. He'll never be with one woman, and certainly not me. I know that, but it's hard not to catch feelings when we do what we do. I want him for myself. I can never say how I really feel because it would ruin the good time we are having. Nothing kills fun faster than 'I love you.' I'm pretty sure he'd stop seeing me and I don't want that. No, I'm better off taking what little I can and being happy with that. It's for the best.

Jack is rinsing the shampoo out of my hair and I look up at him through my lashes like he's a dream, in awe of his immense beauty. My heart races as he touches me, holds me, cares for me.

"What's that look, Rosey?"

I look away. "What? Nothing." Shit. He caught me.

"Hmm." He turns off the water and wrings the water from my hair. He steps out first and grabs a towel for me, wrapping it around me. "Not gonna tell me," he says, almost to himself.

"I said it was nothing," I reply, drying off my legs.

Suddenly, he scoops me up and carries me to the bedroom. He falls onto the bed, taking me with him. At first, it feels playful, so when Jack grabs my hands I willingly wrap my fingers around his. It feels like we're having a moment. My heart pitter-patters in my chest, thinking that he's giving me a little of the sweetness that I crave. Then I feel cool metal against my wrists and hear a snap. Instantly my blood goes cold. Oh shit. What have I done? My eyes are wild and afraid.

He's kneeling over me. "You shoulda told me when I asked."

I bite my lip. "It really wasn't anything, Jack."

He moves quickly to fasten my ankles to each bedpost. He rips the towel out from under me.

"Jack, you don't need to—"

He interrupts me with a hand over my mouth, a second later he stuffs my panties into it, thereby stopping any further communication. He grabs my wide belt from the floor, then kneels next to me again. He fastens it around my head, covering my eyes. I may have underestimated this situation. I didn't know he'd get so upset. There's nothing I can do now. I know him. Now he's going to punish me into submission.

I feel something tickling my belly, grazing my chest. It feels cool, firm, and smooth. He must be touching me with some kind of object. It suddenly slaps against my tender skin and I let out a muffled shriek. My heart is pounding in my ears.

I feel the bed dip as he moves in by my ear. "It's nothing," he repeats, as something slaps against my thigh. It stings. I give a muffled cry through the panties in my mouth. I feel something smooth stroking my side. Suddenly it's gone and I ready myself for the slap. I shriek as it hits my pussy. The bed dips as he moves. His big finger teases my open-ing. "Is this nothing?" he asks before slamming his finger into me. I let out a muffled cry. I shake my head no and moan through my panties. How can something so intense—almost violent—feel so good?

I'm quickly reaching the peak of ecstasy when he stops. The bed moves as he gets off of it. Not being able to see what he's doing, I listen intently. I hear his bare feet pad across the floor, a drawer opens and closes. Next thing I hear is a buzzing sound—a vibrator! This is torture. He's next to me again. Slowly, he rubs the vibrator against my pussy, teasing me, keeping it away from where I want it the most. I pull against my restraints.

"Is this nothing too?" he says as he slides it inside me.

I gasp. My back arches and I try to press my hips into it. I need release, some type of friction. I'm so desperate. Jack switches it to pulse as the vibrator hits my G-spot. My pleas go unheard. My whole body is tense and shaking. Just when I'm nearing the edge, he pulls it out, making me groan. "It's nothing," he whispers in my ear.

How long is he going to torture me? I need release.

The vibrator zips in and out until I fear I'll lose consciousness. Then it's gone. Everything is quiet. Next thing I know my belt is removed from my eyes and he takes my panties out of my mouth. My throat is dry. "I'm sorry," I squeak out. "I should have just told you, but I was embarrassed. I was admiring you, that's all. You-you're just so beautiful."

He's zipping up his pants. "Beautiful, huh?"

"Yeah. I was looking up at you and, I don't know,

maybe I liked the way you were caring for me. I just felt some kind of way." I look away as tears prick my eyes.

He releases my feet from the restraints. "Not gonna happen, Rosey."

"I know. God, I know... I'm sorry. I didn't mean..."

He frees my wrists. "Time to go." He gives me the look. The one I always dread. He doesn't allow houseguests. Ever. I rub my wrists and get up. I'm still hot and bothered from the vibrator and our intense interaction, but I reluctantly put my clothes on anyways.

I'm standing in the room, fully dressed, with my jacket draped over my arm. Without a word, he leads me downstairs and to the front door. "I'm really sorry, Jack." I turn and walk down the steps. The door creaks shut, closing with a thud. No matter how much I wish he'd let me in, confide in me, I know he won't.

If I'm going to make it through this, I need to push my feelings aside. Jack's a complicated beast. The last thing I need is to think I'm the one who can tame him. He's in charge, no matter what little bit of power he may choose to give me. He made that crystal clear tonight and I'm never forgetting it again.

# THE CHASE

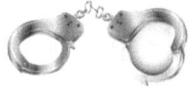

Rosey's in the middle of my candle-lit bedroom wearing nothing but black lace panties and a push-up bra. Her long wavy hair falls over her shoulders. She's so fucking hot and I wanna rub my face between those juicy tits. My eyes take in every inch of her creamy skin with wild abandon. I can't wait to touch her, bite her, punish her, and fuck all her pretty little holes.

Ever since she punished me, she's been insatiable. I've finally unleashed the beast. When I first laid eyes on her, I knew there was a caged animal inside her, and I wanted to set it free. Now that I have, I only want more. I gave her a little more freedom tonight, just to see where it would lead. I eye her carefully from the doorway, wondering what plan she's conjuring up in her dirty little mind. My dick is throbbing with anticipation.

Her eyes are dark and wild. Her beautiful tits pop as her chest heaves. "I want..."

"Tell me."

"I want... I want you to chase me."

My eyes widen. "What?"

"I want to run and have you chase me."

I cross my arms and lean against the door frame. "Really?" I say with a smirk.

She nods.

My heart is thrumming in my chest. "How does that work?"

She licks her lips. "Well, you'll give me a head start."

"And then?"

"Then, you'll come after me." She bites her bottom lip.

My heart rate increases and adrenaline is coursing through my veins. Chasing her, catching her, claiming her—this is exactly what I want, and she's serving it up on a slutty silver platter for me. I swallow hard. "And when I catch you?"

She takes a step toward me, grinning. "*If* you catch me."

I stand up straight, arms by my side. I'll play along. "Okay, *if* I catch you?"

One more step towards me, as she bites her bottom lip. "Then you can do what you want with me."

I unbutton my light blue dress shirt. "You better fucking run fast," I growl, shifting my shirt off my shoulders and setting it aside. "Safe word?"

"Cinnamon," she replies, staring up at me through her dark eyelashes.

I take off my socks for better traction. "Ready." I grab her upper arms and spin her around so she's facing the open door. She glances back at me, wanting reassurance. "Better be ready to move."

"I will be." She steps her right foot forward and hunches down like she's at a starting block. Her perfect ass on display in her little see-through panties. I like this game already.

"I'm gonna give you to the count of three."

She nods.

"One," I say slowly.

She takes off, darting out of the room.

"Two." I call after her. I'm imagining how her heart is beating out of control, her adrenaline coursing through her veins. The corners of my mouth curl, so excited for the chase. Fuck, this girl.

I hear her feet thud as they hit the steps. She's running downstairs, like a little deer in the woods, trying to escape the hunter on her tail. I yell out, "Three!"

My predator instincts kick in and I lunge forward, racing into the hall and jumping down the stairs—three at a time. Her fear is potent in the air. I lick my lips. When I catch up, she's behind the couch. She runs left and I follow. Suddenly she shifts directions and I jump over the back of the couch.

"Jack!" she shrieks.

I chase her around the coffee table. Her eyes are big and wild, her chest is heaving. I'm calm—deadly calm. It won't be long before I catch her, but I like to play with my food. I reach out for her, intentionally missing, just so I can drive up the intensity of her fear. She nearly falls as she makes a break for it, running past the table and heading towards the couch. I let her go. She's got nowhere to go but upstairs or outside, and I know she won't choose the latter. I hear her feet padding up the stairs. I run after her calling, "Rosey..."

When I get to the landing at the top of the stairs, I turn right and open the door of the spare bedroom. She runs around to the other side of the bed. I fake-lunge, making her shriek and hop up onto the bed.

Each move I make is sending her exactly where I want her. My throat rumbles as I prowl back and forth in front of the bed with my muscular arms out to my sides.

"Jack!" she yells, her legs shaking.

I hop onto the bed and she jumps off and heads out the door. This time I won't let her get very far. She's falling right into my plan. I track her as she runs across the hall and into my lair. Now I simply walk across the hall, knowing I've got her where I want her. She's right in front of me, darting around looking for an escape. I grab her arm, pulling her into me. "Got ya." My face in her hair, I inhale deeply, drinking in the scent of fear mingled with her raspberry shampoo.

She tries to wriggle free. "Jack... please." Her heart pounds in her chest. My hard cock is pressed up against her ass.

Without hesitation, I pick her up like she's nothing more than a rag doll. She's fighting me every step of the way but my grip is too strong—she can't get away. The bitch bites my shoulder and I smack her ass. But it's okay. The more she fights, the more this cock is going to destroy her pretty holes. All of her pretty holes.

I close the door behind me, and toss her onto the bed. "Now it's my turn."

She scurries off the bed. I unfasten my belt. Then I unzip my fly and strip my pants and black boxer briefs off. I'm standing stark naked in front of her. I stalk over to her and she tries to get away but I've got her right where I want her. I grab a hold of her arms, pulling her into me. One snap to the back of her bra and it falls to the floor. Her round tits bounce around as she wrestles trying to escape my grasp. She bites my arm. I grab her panties in my hand and rip them off. She curses. "Nothing to hide behind now."

I lift her up and toss her onto the bed again. She scoots back until her back is pressed against the headboard. Her darkened eyes glance down my body, stopping at my throbbing cock.

"See something you like?" I give it a few rough tugs. "You like watching me stroke this cock?"

She bites her lip.

"Answer me."

"Yes," she moans quietly.

I stalk towards the bed and she scrambles towards the edge. "Nowhere to go, Rosey. The only way out is the door and I'm guarding it with my life." I grab her by the ankles, yanking her towards me. I make a circle in the air. "Turn around, feet facing away from me. I'm gonna throat fuck you while I eat your sweet little pussy."

She gasps and quickly maneuvers around so her head is just off the edge of my bed. "Good girl."

My dick is throbbing and dripping by her head. I scan her body—she looks so fucking good. I lean forward, brushing my hands over her breasts, giving them a squeeze. I slide further down, spreading her open and teasing her clit with my thumb. "Mmm..." My cock is so hard it's about to pop. I need to feel her lips wrapped around it.

Without warning, I thrust it partway into her mouth with a groan. She gurgles a moan. I thrust a few more times and pull out. My attention goes back to her. I give her sweet pussy a few light slaps. "Ahh!" she cries as her back arches.

"You like that?"

She nods. "Uh-huh."

I thrust into her again. This time a little further. "I'm surprised how well you take this cock," I groan, watching my dick disappear into her mouth.

Back to her. Time to give my girl a little satisfaction. As I thrust, I dive into her pussy with my tongue. She makes a muffled sound, too much dick in her mouth to do more. I lick her opening, dipping my tongue inside. She gurgles. A few more thrusts. I want to go in balls deep, but I don't know if she can handle it. I suck on her clit and she suddenly grabs my hips, pulling me deeper into her mouth. She nearly chokes, tears streaming her cheeks, but she keeps going. My little trooper. She pulses back and forth at the back of her throat. "Fuck, you feel so good." Shivers break out over my body. The ache is growing. "Ahh, shit you're gonna make me cum," I groan.

Rosey's doing such a good job—she really is—but I can't cum in her mouth. I pull my dick out of her mouth and a thick string of saliva follows. She struggles to catch her breath. Mascara tears stream down her face, but she doesn't even try to wipe them away.

"Good girl," I say, brushing her silky hair with my hand. "I'm gonna pleasure you." I slap her pussy lightly and her back arches. With my tongue I tease her pussy, licking her juicy wet lips, dipping into her center.

"Fuck," she moans.

I spit on her pussy before diving back in and sucking on her clit. She's clutching the comforter as her body writhes underneath me. Another slap on her pussy. I take her clit in my teeth.

She arches off the bed, lifting her hips. "Unh…"

I stick one of my big fingers inside her and she's done. She moans and screams as she grips my finger, cumming all over it. I lick up the spoils. She tastes so good.

Panting, her eyes half-closed, my girl tries to put my dick back into her mouth. I love that she's trying.

I chuckle. "No, Rosey… this load is meant for your tight little asshole." Her eyes widen. When I go to flip her over, she resists again. In a sudden burst of adrenaline, she quickly scrambles to get away from me. Admittedly, she caught me off guard so she manages to make it off my bed. In one movement, I jump onto my mattress, grabbing her before her little ass goes any further.

"Fuck!" she squeals.

I cover her mouth with one hand, the other one acts as a vice grip holding her in place. I press my hard cock against her ass, as I whisper in her ear, "I guess we're doing this the hard way."

She gives a muffled shriek and twists her body away, fighting me every step of the way. I turn her around and pin her face down into the bed. Her whole body is shaking, which makes it even better. "I was gonna lick your little asshole before I fucked it, just to lube you up. But now, I'm going in without it."

She lifts her head trying to get up but I have her pinned really well. I wrap my arms around her waist. "Hips up." She squirms again. "Don't make it any harder than it needs to be." She's on her knees, ass in the air. My right hand pressing her shoulders down. "You ready for me?"

She nods.

"Tell me."

"I'm ready."

I line the tip of my cock up with her puckered hole. "What are you ready for?"

"Your cock... give it to me... please."

"That's more like it." That earns her a little reprieve. I spit and it lands right on her asshole. I rub it in with my thumb, teasing her hole as I do. Once she's good and lubed up, I press the tip of my cock into her puckered hole.

She winces. "Ahh..."

"You like that?"

Rosey's body is shaking as she nods.

I clamp down even harder than before and thrust myself into her, forcing my entire cock into her ass.

"Fuck," she cries.

I lean in closer. "Now this is the part where I fuck you till *I* cum." I thrust into her tight little asshole, slowly at first, but I'm so hard and horny, it isn't long before I'm hitting it hard.

"Please..." she moans.

I groan as I pound into her. It's so primal and animalistic—holding her down, fucking the shit out of her. She's had me turned on for so long I know I can't last much longer. That tight little asshole is gripping my cock like it's trying to squeeze the cum right out of me. I pull her in tighter with my arm wrapped around her throat.

She moans, "Harder..."

Sweat covers my back as I give her everything I've got—thrusting in balls deep and back out before pounding into her again. She's taking me so well. "I'm gonna fill your little ass with my cum." Goosebumps erupt over my skin and my body bucks as I let go. "Fuck," I grunt. Everything I have spurts out inside her. "Oh... shit... ahh." My cock pulses and quivers as it finishes releasing inside her. "I just fucking came up your ass."

My shoulders slump and I loosen my grip on her. She looks as satisfied as I feel. Her eyes are half-closed, like she's in a sex induced daze. "You did so well," I say, rubbing her ass. I look down and pull my cock out of her slowly. Some of my cum seeps out of her little hole and dribbles down her ass and pussy, soaking the comforter below. The corners of my mouth twist into a wicked smile as I admire my work, the masterpiece that I just created. I spread her cheeks open, getting a good look before I take her to the shower.

Damn.

This dirty little cum slut dripping on my bed is the most beautiful sight I've ever fucking seen.

# JACK MARSHALL & MEL BELLAMY

## THE SEXTING

### JULY 2024

My day was long and taxing, sitting in a hot car all day on a stake-out. It's no fun being a PI sometimes. All I want to do is relax. I'm sprawled out on the sectional with a beer bottle up to my lips when my phone pings. I lean over to pick it up off the side table.

> MEL: unreasonably hungry...

I toss the phone onto the couch like it's on fire. That's one chick I don't want to hear from. I'm a good judge of character, and Mel, she's fucking crazy. The night we met, she stalked me all night and told me her *whole* drunken life story. Not only did I have to hear her slurred rendition of why daddy doesn't love her, she spilled her red wine all over me. She's a tattooed, pierced, tom-boy, who's pushy, arrogant, and doesn't know where the line is—not my type *at all*.

That night, after she insisted on having my stained shirt dry-cleaned, she grabbed my phone out of my hand and added herself as a contact, then texted herself so she'd have my number. The worst kind of girl—the worst. And why's she reaching out now? She never did pay for my dry cleaning. She seems drunk and she probably is. My phone pings again. Against my better judgment, I grab it.

MEL: hello... big guy?

Big guy? Does she even know who she's texting? Probably not. Remember, she's crazy and possibly drunk. But my dick twitches of its own accord. What does 'unreasonably hungry' mean? I know I shouldn't reply, but my fingers type a response anyway.

JACK: for?

She sends an eggplant emoji.

Fuck, that shouldn't turn me on but it does. I

mean, she's not my type, but still hot. I can picture her; she's a tiny little thing, 5'4 on a good day with a massive round ass. But then again, there's that full tat sleeve, the septum piercing, a purple streak in her wavy dark shoulder-length hair. I need to steer clear of her. That's what I should do. My dick twitches in my trousers, remembering that juicy ass of hers. Never seen anything like it. I set my beer down on the glass coffee table in front of me and type out a response.

> JACK: mmm sounds like you need some dick

I pause before sending. This is a horrible idea. She's nuts. I gather my senses and try to delete my message, but my big, stupid thumb hits the send button instead. Three little dots appear immediately. Fuck. What have I done?

> MEL: being single sucks

Without pause, my dick takes over and starts typing.

> JACK: single huh?

MEL: yup

JACK: i'd give you this dick

Bad idea. This whole thing is a bad idea.

MEL: too bad you're so far away

JACK: why... where are you?

MEL: baton rouge... business

Again, I type with my fully hard dick-brain.

JACK: bet you'd cum hard for me too

For every sane idea that I have, my dick does the opposite. He's throbbing in my tight pants wondering what she's going to say next—we both are. Once again, the three little dots appear.

MEL: so fucking hard

Shit. My blood-pressure sky-rockets. The thought of claiming her ass and being the one who makes her cum. I'm in trouble.

MEL: not only would I cum hard for you, i'd be as loud as fuck

I'm getting the sex sweats.

JACK: fuck... i'd love to hear that... i want you to cum so fucking hard your legs shake

I unzip my fly and pull my throbbing dick out of my pants, giving it a few rough tugs.

MEL: damn boy, what are you trying to do to me?

JACK: everything

MEL: fuck

JACK: my kink is making women cum

MEL: really?

JACK: yea, when you tell me you're horny i can't stop

MEL: so don't then... (the longest foreplay in history)

> JACK: look at you… so hungry
> to cum

> MEL: every fucking second of every
> fucking day

I settle back into the couch, jerking off in between typing. I drop the phone a few times trying to do both.

> JACK: if i was there, i'd make you
> cum until you couldn't anymore

> MEL: wanna video chat… need to
> see that D

I chuckle. This girl. I may know this is a bad idea but I can't quit. I run my hand through my hair before I hit the call button. It rings a couple of times before she picks up. When she answers, I see her tits before I see her face. A black silk bralette highlighting her perky mounds. My mouth waters as I imagine biting into them. Finally, she shifts the angle of her phone, possibly putting it on a stand. That's what I should have done. I glance around for something to lean my phone against but don't have an easy solution so I continue to hold it.

"Hey, big guy," Mel says with a crooked smile.

I grunt. That smile. Those jade-hued eyes.

"You're smokin' hot," I reply. Even if I'm going to regret this later, it's too late now. I'm all in.

She tucks her hair behind her ear. "Am I? You're the one who looks like a demi-god." I chuckle. She's funny. I'm about to respond when she says, "Now show me that D."

I run my hand over my stubbled chin. "Desperate for the dick, aren't you?"

She inhales deeply, her eyes staying closed for a second before she opens them again. "You have no idea."

I guess I'm doing this. I stretch backwards and hold the phone up so she gets a good look at my cock, then quickly move the camera back up to my face.

Her eyes widen. "Jeezus! Where have you been hiding that monster?"

I snicker.

"Big guy, I'm gonna need some of that." She licks her lips.

"Yea, but you're gonna need to make yourself cum, since I can't be there."

She rolls her eyes. "Yeah, I know how this works."

"Did you just roll your fucking eyes?"

"Yeah, I did," she replies with both attitude and nonchalance.

"Hmm..."

I remain quiet for a while. She eyes me carefully before speaking. "What does that mean?"

"Gonna need to punish you."

"Oh yeah?" she says flippantly.

"Have to see if you can be a good girl." The thought of punishing her, tying her up, spanking her is making me as hard as a rock. My cock is aching.

"Ha! I'd like to see you try and make me!" she screeches.

"Hanging up..."

She holds her hand up and waves it in front of her. "Wait, hold on. Don't be so rushy. Like, what do I need to do?"

"Behave," I growl.

"Fuck... okay, I'll try to behave."

I smirk, such a little brat. "*Try*?"

She smiles coyly. "You caught that, huh?"

I nod. "Get on your knees and beg for this cock." I flash her my dick again, this time stroking it for her.

"Fuck, jeezus... that fucking cock."

"Beg."

She sighs and her face scrunches up. "Why don't you bring me to my knees if that's what you want."

"Cause if you want it bad enough, you'll fall to your knees without me even asking."

She glances away. "Oh, it's like that huh. Hard pass."

"I'll just find someone who will and make you watch."

"If that's supposed to be a threat, you don't know me very well," she scoffs.

This is gonna be more fun than I thought. "Show me your tits."

She twists her arms behind her back as she unfastens her bra, then moves the angle of the camera. A moment later I'm staring at her perfect tits, dreaming about cumming all over them. "Fucking hot."

"You stroking that big cock?" She licks her lips.

"Yeah, wanna see?"

"Yes."

I show her how hard I am, the pre-cum that's gathering on my tip making my dick glisten. I stroke it a few times, letting her watch. "Mmm.... fuck..."

Her chest is heaving as she exhales loudly.

"Now, get on your fucking knees and take this dick."

"Okay, give it to me then."

Still rubbing my cock, I groan, "You need to earn it."

"Fuck, okay... I'll behave..."

"Beg."

She sighs. "Please give me your cock, daddy."

"Not very convincing."

"Please, I need it. Fuck, I need your cock. Please..."

I groan. "That's better. Now be a good girl and fit my big fucking cock in your mouth."

"Okay, daddy... I'll take it all..."

"Open wide and put your fingers in your mouth. I'm gonna fuck your pretty little throat."

"Mmm..." Her tongue slides up her middle finger and she sticks it in her mouth. Her cheeks hollow as she sucks on it, like she's sucking on my cock. *Fuck.* With hooded eyes, she dips her fingers in and out of her mouth. She whimpers and drool pools at the corners of her mouth. I give her a little treat and hold the camera so she can see me stroking my cock.

She gives a garbled groan.

"Let me see your tongue as you lick your fingers." Mel does as I ask and I see something glistening in her mouth. "Hold up, what's that?" She sticks her tongue out close to the camera. "Tongue piercing?"

She nods.

"Mmm... I'd love to feel that as you suck my fucking cock."

The corner of Mel's mouth curls.

"Now, get back to work."

"Yes, daddy... mmm, you taste so good... I'm gonna suck your big cock until you cum deep in my throat."

"Damn..." She's bringing me right to the edge. My strokes are rough, aching to cum. "You love that big cock, don't you?

"Yea. I like teasing the tip with my tongue piercing then swallowing you whole."

Such a dirty little cum slut. "I'm gonna fill all your holes... that dirty little mouth is only the beginning." My breathing is ragged.

"Mmm... yes, daddy... I'm all yours."

My body tenses. The ache is unbearable; I need to cum. "Your mouth feels so good. I'm gonna cum." I unbutton my shirt, letting it hang open.

"You feel so fucking good," she moans.

"Where's that other hand, you playing that pretty little pussy?"

She bites her lip and nods.

I groan. "Show me."

Mel reveals her nearly bare pussy—just a little dark strip of hair, glistening with her desire. There's something else. Another piercing, right on her clit—with a vertical barbell sticking straight through the hood. "Damn, that's hot. Touch it for me."

Mel's eyes are nearly closed as she plays with her pierced clit. Her back arches and her chest heaves.

"Cum for me, gorgeous."

"Ahh..." she moans, as her fingers dip into her tight pussy.

That's all it takes to push me to the edge. I quickly hit the audio record and stroke my cock a few more times. "Fuck..." I blow a fat load all over my stomach as she watches.

"Shit... oh god, mmm... ahh..." Her body bucks as she climaxes.

I'm trying to catch my breath. "That was fucking hot."

There's a delicious half-smile on her face. "You're fucking hot."

I chuckle.

"That was fun but I really gotta go," she says finally.

"Ok, dirty girl... later."

I send one final message, the audio clip of us cumming. As soon as I hit send, I get up and go to the bathroom to wash the sticky mess off of me. When I return three dots appear on my screen.

MEL: well, damn... that was the hottest thing I've ever heard

JACK: oh yeah?

My dick twitches.

MEL: yeah.

I was into it, and it was fun, but now that it's over, my sanity has returned. This was probably a huge fucking mistake. But no matter what my brain says, my dick can't stop thinking about her. Her tight pussy, her moans, those piercings and what they'd feel like on my cock. When I'm in the shower, when I'm lying in bed alone—all I think about is her. Her words stick out in my mind 'that was the hottest thing I've ever heard.' She's right; it was.

In the darkened room, my phone lights up and pings. I lean over and pick it up off the nightstand.

MEL: i just came so hard listening to that recording

I chuckle. Damn this girl. My dick twitches in response. I slide my hand under the sheet and rub my growing cock. Now, that will go down in history as the hottest thing anyone's ever said to me. Fuck.

## THE ASS

It's Friday night and I'm at The Sunspot. Girls dancing on poles, $3 beers—life couldn't get any better than this. My buddy, Reggie, just left for the restroom when I see Crazy Mel across the bar. Shit, I don't need this right now. I turn away hoping she doesn't see me. Next thing I know she saunters up to the bar and leans against it. She's so cocky as she stares up at me from her waist high perspective with those green eyes of hers. I can't help but notice the skin-tight black jeans she has on and the cropped gray sleeveless tee, highlighting her tattoos. Every time I look at her, all I think is she's not my type.

So why the fuck am I picturing her bent over with my dick in her ass?

"Hey, big guy," she says with a smirk.

"What's up?" I sip my beer, acting completely disinterested. Though my half-chub might disagree.

She grabs a shot glass from the bar and downs it. "Nothing much," she replies. I'm not even sure that was her drink. Then she waves to the bartender for another. He gives her a refill and she knocks it back too. "You over here trying to ignore me?

"Enh." I shrug, bringing my beer bottle up to my lips,

"Ha! I see, you think I'm going to come onto you cause we sexted once." I sip my beer. "You think you're irresistible, don't you?" Mel draws a line down my arm with her finger seductively and rolls her tongue across her top teeth, ever so slowly. "Mr. Ladies Man." My cock twitches and I press my arm into my crotch trying to hide my bulge. I'm not letting this little girl get to me. Fuck that. I repeat my mantra in my head, 'this bitch is crazy... this bitch is crazy... this bitch is crazy...'

Reggie rejoins me at the bar, saving me from Mel. I chuckle. "Everything turn out alright?"

"Fuck off. Want another?" he asks pointing to his brown beer bottle.

I nod.

Out of the corner of my eye I catch Mel's death

glare. "Wow. You know what, you're a fucking asshole. Whatever." She turns on her heel and leaves with a pronounced huff. I snicker and go back to my beer.

"That little cat got your tongue?" Reggie asks out of nowhere.

"Huh?" I turn my head towards him.

"The pint-size sex-machine," he mocks. "She was clearly trying to get your attention."

I grunt in response.

"Oh, she got under your skin." Reggie nudges me with his shoulder.

"Nah."

His eyebrows raise. "I mean, she is hot."

I groan. "No, she's crazy." Reggie shrugs and starts talking about the game we watched on Sunday —how his team got a touchdown and how much money he made from his pre-game bet, even making fun of my team pick—but all I can think about is her. Her tongue rolling over her teeth, the metal piercing bobbing in her mouth as she talks, the sound she makes when she cums—the sound that I've listened to at least a hundred times since we sexted. My dick is twitching at the thought. This stupid little cunt is in my head and I can't get her out. The only option is to taste her, otherwise I'll never stop thinking about her.

I glance over my shoulder to see where she got off to. It takes me a minute to find her, but when I do, she's in the middle of the dance floor, her arms in the air as she sways her hips, with some dude grinding up against her ass. Her peach of an ass. Her perfectly round, perfectly juicy ass. *Fuck*. I need her. Now. I stand abruptly, my stool scraping against the floor. I abandon my beer and Reggie to go after her. I hear Reggie mocking me as I storm off, but I don't fucking care. I need this little cunt and I'm going to take her.

I don't know if it's my imposing figure or the ferocity with which I'm moving, but the sea of dancing bodies parts as I stalk towards Mel. The second she's within reach I pick her up and throw her over my shoulder.

"Whoa! What do you think you're doing?" The dude that was just grinding on her shoves me—dude with a muscle shirt and gold chains that's gonna get his ass handed to him if he doesn't quit.

I scowl down at him, fists clenched. That's all it takes and he throws his hands up, backing away slowly. "Alright, alright... no problem."

Mel is pounding her tiny fists against me. "Hey!"

Her attempts to assault me are laughable. Muscle shirt guy doesn't intrude again as I carry her across the dance floor. I storm down the dark carpeted hallway leading to the bathrooms. "Put me down, asshole!" she yells, still punching.

Seriously, she's gonna regret all her fucking antics, cause now, I'm gonna fuck the bad girl out of her—and in a dirty club bathroom too. With the palm of my hand, I bust open the door. I slam the door behind me and secure us both inside. No more waiting. No more teasing. I need to be inside her. I set her on the edge of the sink, still restraining her.

"If you behave, I might let you cum."

She rolls her eyes so dramatically I know that I'm gonna take her ass first. This little cunt needs to be taught a lesson. I spin her around so she's facing the mirror.

"What the fuck, dude?"

I hold her against the counter with my body. She's so short her feet barely touch the ground.

I grab her hair and pull her head back. She curses. "Do you want this?" I ask huskily.

"Fuck you, asshole!" she spits.

"Tell me or I put you down right now."

She gives me a slight nod.

"Tell me." My voice is low and raspy.

"Yes, okay... fuck."

"Stand on my feet," I command as I yank down her jeans and panties. Her pretty round ass is now on full display. With my free hand, I slide my fingers into my mouth, covering them with saliva. She's lucky I'm feeling generous. I was gonna fuck her with no lube. I spread her ass cheeks and rub my thumb over her pretty puckered hole. "I'm gonna claim your fucking ass," I whisper near her ear.

She whimpers.

I rub my cock between her ass cheeks. Up and down, squeezing her soft cheeks around me. "Mmm... you feel so good." Damn. I add some extra spit to my cock before I ease into her. Just the tip, but it already feels so good. So fucking good. "Fuck..." I curse. It isn't long before I'm half-way in. She takes me so well. "Ahh... your ass is so fucking tight." Shivers erupt all over my shoulders and back.

"Jeezus, you're big..."

"You can take me."

"Fuck..."

With my free hand I slide down her flat stomach and roll my thumb over her clit. "Ohh...fuck, yeah," she cries out.

"You like that?" I groan.

"Uh-huh."

This needs to be quick and dirty. We're in the bathroom for fuck's sake. "I'm gonna go hard on you now."

She grips the counter with both hands. I grind myself into her, making her groan. In and out as I play with her clit. Harder, faster. I'm so close. Her body tenses and she tosses back her head. "Cum for me," I moan, wrapping my arm around her throat and pulling her into me.

Mel is moaning every inhale, groaning every exhale. Her eyes are hooded, like she's in some other world. I fucking know that look. "Oh god..." she screams as she climaxes. I pound into her ass as I fill her with my cum. Jerking in and out as the last of it pulses into her. "Oh, shit... you feel so good..." I lean back, still holding her against the counter as I catch my breath. "Damn... mmm..."

When I finally recover, I pull out. A wicked smile plays on my lips as I watch my cum dribble down her ass crack. Perfect. I set her down, feet back on the floor. Her eyes are glazed over. "You okay?"

"Yeah... I think you fucked the life out of me though"

I chuckle.

She pulls her panties and jeans back up. "I thought you hated me."

"I do." I zip up.

She turns and washes her hands. "I hate you too," she says, smirking at me in the mirror.

I slap her round ass, hard.

Mel glowers at me. "Let's not do this again."

"No problem." I unlock the door and swing it wide open, leaving her standing there on her own. I'm filled with instant regret. The sex was mind-blowing, but she's right, we shouldn't do it again. I definitely don't want to. She's crazy. Crazy good.

## MEL BELLAMY

Today has been a scorcher, and my apartment doesn't have AC, so I'm hanging out in the freezer section of Eddy's Market. In only my black crop top and cut off shorts, I shouldn't still be this warm. The frozen peas I have on the back of my neck are starting to cool me down. Suddenly, there's a crashing sound, and I turn to see what happened. Down at the end of the aisle, I see Jack, the ass. He's holding his hands up as a gray-haired woman scolds him. I scowl just looking at him. Why is it that every time I turn around, there he is? Should I leave now or harass him a little first? I'm hot and cranky, the choice is practically made for me.

I saunter up to him. "So, big guy, you following

me?" He tries to move past me, but I block him. I bring my hand up to my mouth and half-whisper, "I mean, the last time I saw you, you pummeled my ass with your giant dick." I poke his giant, muscley arm.

He cracks his knuckles.

"Maybe what you really want..." I step closer to him, "is to fuck me in this grimy grocery store bathroom." I run my finger down the center of his chest and he growls a warning. "What you really want is to rip off my clothes and punish me." For extra emphasis, I grind my body into his. My initial goal was to torture him, but now everything I'm saying is turning me on. I'm so desperate for his big D.

He pushes my body away. "Enough."

Anyone else would probably heed his warning, but instead I poke my finger into his chest. "Oh, got under your skin, did I?" His fists make a loud cracking noise and I glance down. It isn't just his big hands that I see. He's got a full on boner. I know I got to him now. Time to turn up the heat. "No problem. I'll just leave you alone then." I bring out the full catwalk strut, swinging my ass as I do. I love to fuck with him, but it's like riding a double-edged sword. Truly, he's the kind of guy that I hate—big, musclebound, and full of himself, and yet I also crave his dick. I'm probably going to regret messing with him today. The tension I feel behind me lets me know that I'm about to get fucked, and really hard too.

Suddenly, his giant arm wraps around my waist and he flings me over his shoulder. He gives my ass a proper smack as he stalks down the aisle and out the front door. He doesn't seem to give two shits who sees either. We're out the door and into the thick summer evening heat, then over to his black mustang—even his car is pure testosterone. With a click of the handle, he opens the door, folds the driver's seat forward and tosses me into the back seat, literally. Asshole.

"Hey!"

Jack-ass returns his seat to upright and slides in. He turns the car on, revving it as he closes his door.

"What the fuck do you think you're doing?" I screech.

He shifts the car into gear and peels out of his parking spot and through the lot.

"Where are you taking me?" I try again.

He drives into an alleyway that's free of street lamps and parks next to the building. It's so fucking hot in this car. He's in a button-down shirt with the sleeves rolled up, but he must be roasting. He does look yummy though.

He stares at me from the rearview mirror. "Take

your shorts off." I unzip them and take them and my panties off. "On my lap. Now." There's something about the way he orders me around. I jump the second he gives me a command. I climb between the seats and straddle him. He glides his hands up my back and into my hair. Oh god, I love how he touches me. "You like teasing me, little cunt."

I smirk. "A little."

He grabs my hair, using it to pull back my head. "Ahh..."

"Well, now you're gonna pay."

My head is locked in place, but I try to nod.

"Take my dick out." I scramble to unzip his pants, grabbing a hold of his thick cock. My hands look tiny next to him. I swallow hard. "Slide on."

I lift up onto my knees, then scoot down on top of him. I'm so fucking wet already, he slips in easily, despite his size. He sucks his teeth and groans. He wraps his fingers deeper into my hair. His other hand grips my hip, pressing me downward.

"Shit, I forgot about your anaconda, jeezus..."

He snickers and licks his lips. "Take in every fucking inch of me."

He lifts his hips towards me, while pushing my body down. "Fuck!" I moan. He's filling me so completely that I swear he's rearranging my insides.

The big guy leans back and stares at my pussy, watching his big cock destroy me. I tighten around him, intentionally pulsating to send him over the edge. His body tenses and he curses, "Fuck... you feel so good."

My orgasm is smacking me in the face as I bounce up and down on him. I'm so drunk on this D. My nipples are over-stimulated, I need friction now. As if reading my thoughts, he leans in and bites my right nipple through my top. "Unh... oh... fuck... again." He grabs a hold of my breast and sucks on it, cotton tee and all. That's it for me. "Oooh, fuck..."

A few more solid thrusts and he grunts, "Unh..." He grabs my hips, his body jerking as he spurts inside me.

Another orgasmic wave and he's sending me over the edge again. "Goddamn... oh, fuck... mmm... ahh..."

He slumps forward, resting his hand on my thigh. I'm trying to catch my breath. "You trying to kill me with that thing? I swear it was gonna tear me apart."

He leans back against the seat and chuckles. "Funny." He gives my leg a tap and I hop off of him and into the passenger seat. My shorts and panties are a reach away, so I grab them from the back seat.

As I'm dressing, I ask, "How does this keep happening?"

He shrugs as he zips up.

I push my hand into my pocket to rearrange my shorts. "I mean, I really can't stand you," I say with a smirk.

"Can't stand you either," he replies, rolling down the window. "You're fucking crazy."

My blood instantly boils. "Oh, I'm crazy?" I give him an exaggerated eye roll. "You're the one who threw me over your shoulder and carried me out of the store so you could fuck me in the parking lot," I scoff.

He shakes his head. "Crazy bitch."

"Jack-ASS!" I spit, my anger is getting the better of me. I swing open the passenger door and get out. Then I lean over, placing one hand on the top of the door and glare at him. "I *never* want to see you again."

"Ditto."

I slam the door with a satisfying *bang*! I storm off, cursing the day that I ever ran into him, pissed at myself for allowing him to get to me, wishing I didn't just fuck him *again*, hating myself for how much I loved it. The only good thing is imagining that he's watching my ass as I walk away. Cause if I know anything, that's exactly what he's doing. I smack my own ass. It can't hurt to put a little more sway in those hips, sticking out that booty. I'm not even back to my car yet when I'm thinking about that D again. It seriously needs its own zip code. If only the anaconda wasn't attached to Jack-ass. But as it stands, I'm well and truly fucked.

# JACK MARSHALL & HELENA CARTER

## THE SEX CLUB
### AUGUST 2024

Walking through the glass doors of the upscale sex club, I see her at the bar sipping a martini. She's perched on a white leather low-back bar stool with a gold frame. Helena. She's all legs and desire. We've been 'friends' for a few years now. One of the only women I've ever met that doesn't get emotionally attached. In a way, she's perfect. Besides she's got to be one of the hottest chicks I've ever seen. Model height with silky, dark shoulder length hair, chocolate hued eyes so dark they always look like they're blown out, and those juicy red lips—it's hard not to imagine them wrapped around my cock.

Helena catches a glimpse of me and flashes her signature smile—elegant with perfect white teeth.

Her vibe is almost cavalier, like she knows how stunning she is. Her fitted red dress is draped low, highlighting her perky tits. Fuck. Her dress is short, almost too short, another inch and the room would see her peach of an ass.

"Jack." She gives me a kiss on each cheek.

I pull her into me by her waist, squeezing her ass with my hand. "Gorgeous."

"Do you want a drink?" she purrs, motioning to the bartender.

I smirk. "Nah." I run my finger down the middle of her chest, barely grazing her tits. "I want to be clear-headed when I fuck the shit out of you."

"Mmm... well, let me finish mine." She reaches for her drink.

I grab a hold of her wrist. "Let's go."

"Jack..." she insists.

I yank her arm once. She shuts up and falls in line. Good girl. I lead her across the bar and over to the playroom door. I'm not in the mood for waiting. It's her fault. That dress—all I can think about is bending her over and fucking her pretty pussy. My cock is already aching and needs relief. Now.

Standing just outside the playroom, I pull Helena into me. "Safe-word?"

Her head bobbles left to right as she says, "Fuck. Off," with a smirk.

I chuckle, brushing her soft cheek with the back of my hand. "Maybe pick something you aren't likely to say later."

Her chest is heaving. "Cocksucker," she hisses. Helena gets off on being volatile, angry, and unhinged before getting railed. This is just the beginning.

I squeeze her tighter. "Helena..." I warn her.

Her eyes are wild. "Bastard. Asshole. Mother-fucker." She twists her arm, trying to free her wrists.

I push her against the wall in front of the door-way, grabbing her by the chin. "Little cunt, give me your safe-word or I'm going to go fuck someone else and make you watch."

She sneers. "Fuck. *You!*" she screeches with emphasis on the latter.

That's it. Her slim wrists tightly in my grasp, I shove the swinging doors open and drag her ass through. The electronic, seductive beat goes straight to my groin. That along with a room full of writhing bodies, tongues on pussies, dicks being sucked— there's a heavy scent of sex in the air. Flashing purple and red strobe lights overhead heighten the mood. I'm filled with need and desire. I scan the room looking for someone to play with. So many beautiful women, a sea of tits and ass, most of whom are engaged with others. My eyes go right to her—a cute little blonde in a short, cream colored tube dress that barely holds in her big tits. Perfect. Our eyes meet and she flashes a smile.

"What are you doing?" Helena asks, struggling to free herself.

I give her a side-glance, growling audibly. I yank on her wrists and stalk across the dim room towards my future playmate. The closer that I get, the harder I become. Helena's pulling and twisting trying to get out of my grasp. Good luck. I'm like a vice grip. There's no way I'm letting her go.

The little blonde is rubbing her thighs together as I approach. It looks like she has an itch that needs to be scratched. I have just the remedy. She plays with one of her long curls. "Hey," she says, shimmying closer to me. Her scent is like an aphrodisiac —amber and sex—my favorite combination.

With the music thumping, there's no way she'll hear me. I lean down and whisper my plan in her ear. Her eyes widen and she whispers back her agreement. "Name?" I ask.

"Lana," she says with a smile.

"Beautiful."

Helena puts up a fight again. I yank on her hand, staring down at her. She immediately stops. She swallows hard, her chest heaving. She knows what's about to happen. If I know her, she's creaming in her panties right now. Fuck. I'm so wired.

Helena by my side, I look down at little blonde Lana. "Beg."

Her eyes are all pupils. "Please, daddy." She drops to her knees in front of me. Her big blue eyes staring up at me. "Let me suck your cock."

I was going to fuck her, but I like where her head is at. Helena tries to pull away, once again. I yank her back to me. "Nope. You're going to stand right here while Lana sucks the cum out of me."

"Fucker!" she hisses.

I turn my attention back to Lana. "Take it out," I command.

Immediately, she unbuckles my belt, unzips my pants, and pulls out my hard cock. She looks to me for instructions, like the good little cum slut that she is. "Suck it."

Lana licks the precum off the tip of my cock, making me groan. It's a thousand times hotter with Helena watching. Lana wraps her red lips around my cock, swallowing me whole. "Fuck..." I moan, licking my lips. Oh, god it feels so good. Her cheeks hollow as she sucks me off. Her tongue sliding up and down my shaft. My cock is deep in her throat, but I still grab the back of her head with my free hand and push myself in further. No fucking gag reflex. "Ahh... oh, fuck..." Lana's sucking on the tip when I turn to Helena and say, "Guess you should've used your safe word." Helena leans into me, her teeth grazing my upper arm. I grab her face and shift her focus back to my cock. "Naw, you're gonna watch this little bitch suck daddy's cock."

She squirms, rubbing her thighs together. "Unh... fuck."

It feels so wicked and I'm ready to blow. Lana goes in harder, sucking my cock like a champ. My body goes stiff and I grunt as I cum into this little cunt's mouth. Helena grips my hand and lets out a feral moan. Lana licks me clean. When she's done, I take her hand and pull her up from her knees.

"Did you like that, daddy?" Lana asks, wiping spit from her chin.

I nod. "Yeah, I fucking did. Such a good girl." I pat her blonde head. I whisper something in her ear and she smiles. She turns and walks off with a skip in her step.

Helena stands on her toes and whispers in my ear. "Dollhouse... my safe word is dollhouse."

"That's more like it." Luckily, my refractory period is short. I scoop her up in my arms and take her to the stage used for performance artists. My voice is low and husky. "I'm gonna fuck you right here."

Helena bites her lip.

I set her down so her feet are in the center of the stage. Her body is close to mine, her wrists restrained behind her back. I motion up at the spotlight overhead. Helena glances upwards, then swallows hard. "Everyone's going to watch while I take your fucking ass."

"Fuck off," she spits.

I chuckle. "And that's why we don't use that as a safe word."

Her chest is heaving and she looks like she wants to kill me. Perfect. "I'm going to bend you over and fill you with this cock."

"I hate you!"

"Oh, you hate me." I spin her around so my cock is pressing into her ass. "Well, you aren't going to hate this dick."

I push her neck forward, bending her over. Fighting me is pointless. She's in this now. That being said, I need to be vigilant, if I lose control of her, she will hit me—and her backhand is no joke. I work her dress up past her hips. No panties. Damn, girl. Seeing her like this, completely spread open is getting me hot. I'm gonna need that pussy in my mouth before I do anything else. I lean down, holding her in place, my tongue lashing out to taste her.

"Mmm..." she moans.

"You like this do you, little cum slut?" I tease her clit with my thumb and run my tongue from her little asshole to her opening. She tastes so good, but I need inside her. Now. "You wet for me?" I slip my fingers into her opening. She's dripping. I work two fingers inside her, pushing in and out, hooking my finger around to her G-spot.

Her legs are shaking and she's panting.

"Nope." I pull away. "Guess you should've behaved earlier." I swipe her sweet juices over her puckered hole. "Now I'm going to punish you." One hand is holding her in place, and with the other, I smack her ass *hard*. She cries out. "You going to be a good girl?"

"Fuck you, bastard!" she screams.

I smack her a little harder this time. Her perfect cheeks are now flushed and pink. "How about now?"

"Never!"

I unzip my trousers and pull out the beast. "Up to

you. I'll just fuck the bad girl out of you then, little cunt."

I lean over and spit on her asshole from above for extra lube. I spit one more time. This one drips down her crack. Perfection. I rub my cock against her puckered hole. "You like that?" Our dirty little show is gathering a crowd. I do like a performance. "I'm gonna claim your ass, while everyone watches."

Helena groans and struggles to break free. I tease her pussy, sliding in a finger, then two. She's so wet. I swipe my soaked fingers against her ass, rubbing her hole, thrusting my dick in between her legs. When she gets really worked up, I know it's time. I lick my lips, enjoying the site of my big cock getting stuffed into her little asshole. "You're so fucking tight." I grab her hips and thrust harder, faster. I throw my head back, feeling so fucking feral. She whines and moans. I lose myself in her, in the erotic feeling. The leering audience pushes me into a sexual daze and I wrap my hand around Helen's throat. "I'm gonna fucking blow a huge load inside you."

"Ahh... do it motherfucker..." she cries.

I pull out almost all the way before slamming into her. I'm so close, right on the edge. Sweat pours down the side of my face. I smack her ass cheek just before plunging into her again. Her ass pulsates around me. I'm balls deep in her as my dick explodes. My body jerks as I fill her ass with my load. "Fuck... aah... goddamn." I slump forward, finally free of the built up tension. I'm breathing heavily as I say, "I just came in your fucking ass."

In my relaxed state, I'm not holding on as tight. Helena thrusts back an elbow nearly catching me in the head. "Cocksucker!" she screams.

I get out of the way just in time. I chuckle as I reinstate my grip. "Oh, did you want to cum?" She wriggles under me. The truth is, I'm nowhere near done with her. I'm gonna punish her all night. If she's lucky she'll get off. No guarantees. I hold her head down and pull my dick out of her. A warm stream of fluid flows out of her hole. It drips down and spills onto the floor. My mouth curls into an evil grin. Perfect. I love to fill her with my cum. She takes it so well.

"Good girl." I shift her dress back down. "Come on, let's go play."

# HELENA CARTER

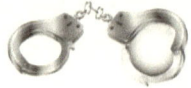

He's pulling me down the dimmed hallway and I'm barely keeping up. His gait is much longer than mine, plus I'm in stilettos. Fucker. Both my wrists are in one hand, like it's nothing to him to hold onto me. I've exhausted myself trying to get away. There's nothing I like more than a good slapping, biting, spitting match. But I know Jack. He isn't into any of that. Even he has his limits. Something about 'if he starts, he may never stop.' Not like I care—I'd love to be smacked right now.

"Jack, slow down," I plead.

He maintains his pace until we reach our destination: a room at the end of the hall, aptly named The Wet Room. Swiping his keycard, he pops open the self-closing door. As soon as we're inside, he slams me up against the wall, his hand around my neck. He's so close I can feel his breath on my face. "Little cunt, misbehaving again."

I try to shake my head no but he's holding me so tight.

"Now I'm gonna punish you." His voice rumbles in my ear. "And you should know, I have no plans on letting you cum."

I let out a low whine.

Jack's hand moves between my thighs, sliding up until he reaches my wet, needy pussy. I moan. His thumb rubs my swollen clit. "This what you want?"

I nod. "Mmm..."

He thrusts one of his big fingers inside me, hooking it around to my g-spot. "Fuck..."

"You like that, little cunt?"

"Yeah."

He grabs the bottom of my dress and hikes it up over my hips. My pussy's on full display for him. I bite my lip with anticipation. "Bet your pussy would love a little tongue action right now."

I swallow hard. "Anh-huh..."

I'm startled when the main door swings open and a tall brunette with blue eyes, wearing nothing but a G-string struts in. She's hot. I've seen her before. Her name's Cassidy and she works at the club, doing exactly what she's about to do—providing pleasure for her customers. She flashes a wicked smile to Jack.

"Sir," she says to him.

Jack still has me pinned to the wall. "My friend here could use a good tongue lashing."

Cassidy winks and nods. "Mmm…"

He grins. "Care to help her out?"

Cassidy licks her lips. "Whatever you need."

I squirm, trying to pull away. Jack strengthens his grip, then spins me around so I'm in front of him. "I'll hold her still for you." He kicks my feet apart, wrapping his legs around mine. He pins me to him with a giant arm across my chest. I can't move, even if I wanted to. "Ready?" he whispers in my ear.

My chest is heaving, heart racing. "Mhmm…"

Cassidy drops to her knees in front of us. She blows on my pussy first, then gently tickles my thighs, all the way up to my hip bone. She licks the crease of my leg with her warm, wet tongue. I inhale sharply. Jack's cock is sticking into my lower back.

"Bring her right to the edge, but don't let her cum."

Cassidy spreads me open with her hands, blowing on me again. She glances up at me as she sticks out her tongue, leans in, and licks my pussy. So fucking hot. My body jerks and I moan, "Oh, fuck."

My legs are shaking as Cassidy continues the assault with her rough tongue. It's when she sucks on my clit that it starts to tip me over the edge. I'm so desperate to cum. I only hope that Jack will let me. So far, he's edged me to insanity. He gets off on punishing me—a trait I usually love. Right now though, Cassidy's masterful tongue-lashing is turning me into putty and I'm about to lose it. "Ahh, fuck... right there..."

That's all Cassidy needs to hear and she stops what she's doing. I watch as she licks my cum off her lips with a slight moan. I would love nothing more than to taste myself on her tongue, kiss her soft lips.

"She's so desperate, isn't she?" Jack asks Cassidy.

She nods. "She is."

He presses his cock into me. "Bet she tastes sweet."

Cassidy's eyes roll into her head. "So fucking sweet."

"Let me taste," he groans.

Cassidy licks me once more, then slips a finger inside me.

My body tenses, legs shaking. "Unh..."

Her finger slides in and out of my pussy a few times, nearly sending me over the edge. She takes her finger out, planting a kiss on my clit. Cassidy stands up, reaching her hand past my head. I follow her hand as she sticks her finger in Jack's mouth and watch as he sucks my cum off of her finger. My pussy is dripping, it's so unbelievably hot. "Mmm..." he moans.

"Please..." I plead, ready to implode.

Jack wraps his arm tighter around my chest and snarls in my ear, "Begging, little cunt? That'll cost you."

"Fuck you!" I scream.

Before I know what's happened, Jack bends me over in front of him and smacks my ass. I moan and he does it again. "You like that?"

"Uh-huh."

Another smack.

"Fuck..." I groan.

Three more smacks, alternating sides. My ass is surely pink by now. He isn't being gentle, which I love. I only wish he was choking me while he was spanking me. I'm so wet and horny that cum is dripping down my leg.

He yanks me up, tossing me over his shoulder. Once we're at the bed, he tosses me onto it. He's held me tight since we arrived at the club, now that I'm free I scurry to the other side of the bed, creating some distance between us. My pulse is racing. I do love a little cat and mouse.

"Not quite, little cunt. I'm not done playing with you yet." He catches a hold of my ankle and pulls me across the bed on my stomach. He smacks my ass. "Dress off." My adrenaline is in overdrive. I'm not even thinking anymore. I twist to release my ankle. Jack immediately pins me to the bed. "Now." He releases my arms so I can sit up and I shift my dress over the top of my head. He tosses it aside.

"Here's what's gonna happen." He restrains my left ankle to the bed with a leather strap. "I'm gonna tie you up." He restrains my right ankle. "And I'm gonna have Cassidy here, bring you to the edge." I glance over at her, nearly forgetting she was still in the room. Meanwhile Jack straps both of my wrists together at the top of the bed. "Again," he rubs my pussy, "and again and again." I squirm and moan, yanking on the restraints. "Don't fucking pull," he warns.

I'm so desperate to cum, I'll do or say anything. "Please... please let me... I'll be good."

Jack motions to Cassidy. "Come here."

She struts over to where he's standing. "Yes, sir."

He flicks her tit and she quivers. "Time to tease that pussy until her legs are shaking."

"Oooh..." I moan loudly.

"But first, why don't you show her what she's missing."

Cassidy nods. "Where do you want me, sir?"

"Suck my cock." Jack hops onto the bed, kneeling right next to me. "Right here."

My whole body convulses. "No... no, please..." I don't even know what I'm pleading for. I'm past my fucking limit. I need to cum. Now. But he won't let me.

Cassidy joins him on the bed. She's on one side of me, Jack's on the other. She unbuckles his belt and takes it off. When she unzips his pants and takes out his cock, I think I'm going to pass out. "Fuck..." My mouth is dry. My pussy's on fire.

He unbuttons his shirt and shifts it off his shoulders. Cassidy grabs his cock and strokes it a few times. He sucks his teeth and groans. The second her mouth envelopes him, I cry out and curse. I pull on my ankle restraints, desperately seeking friction. "Please.... please..."

Jack gives me a laugh. "Looks like you better lick her pussy before she combusts."

Cassidy nods and moves between my legs. She's

about to lick me when he commands, "Don't you dare let her cum."

"Fuck!" I cry out, yanking on my wrist restraints.

Cassidy licks my hip bone, kissing it gently. "Oh, I won't. Only good girls get to cum." She flicks my clit, slapping my pussy. Her tongue feels like heaven—warm, wet, tender, yet rough.

"Mmm..." I moan.

Jack is still kneeling by my side. He picks up his belt. My eyes wide in disbelief. Oh, jeezus what's he going to do to me now? I have a high tolerance for torture and punishment, but he's edging me so hard that I can't function. One smack with that belt and I truly might go up in flames. He grabs the belt with two hands, snapping it a couple of times. The cracking sound makes me sweat and shake.

"Oh, fuck!" I twist and yank on the restraints.

Jack moves closer. "Told you not to pull."

He snaps the tip of the belt across my stomach. "Ahh!"

"You gonna behave?" He doesn't give me a chance to answer before his arm swings back and the belt snaps across my breast, biting my tender skin.

"Ahh," I cry out.

"Move, Cassidy," he commands. She gets out of

the way immediately. "You gonna listen?" he says to me, as the belt snaps against my hip, even biting my pussy. I shriek. Oh god, this feels so fucking good. I feel so alive, every cell awakened. I need more. I need to feel.

My head shakes back and forth as I plead in desperation. "Please, more... harder..."

One more snap to my pussy. Jack's eyes darken. I'm enveloped in his gaze. He looks like he wants to fuck the shit out of me. Good. Fuck me. Fuck me hard. I need it. I need it so fucking bad.

He doesn't break our connection when he says gruffly, "Cassidy, get out. Now." She quickly scurries off the bed and out the door. He straddles my head. "Open your mouth, little cunt."

I open on command and he thrusts his cock into my mouth. "Take this dick, swallow it whole." Oh fuck, he tastes so good. He's fucking my mouth with such aggression, it's nearly making me cum. "Damn, you feel so good." Tears stream down my face, saliva drips from the corners of my mouth. Suddenly he pulls out and I'm left bereft, aching to have his big cock filling me.

"No... no, please..." I whimper.

He pats my head. "You're amazing, but I want to cum in that pretty little pussy."

"Unh..." My whole body quivers.

His hard cock still sticking out of his pants, he moves to the end of the bed, releasing each ankle from the restraints. He rubs my ankles briefly, before bending my legs. His huge body now hovers over the top of me, wasting no time, he slides inside me in one forceful thrust. "Ahh, fuck... you're so fucking wet." He holds one of my knees with his hand and pounds into me.

"Ah... oh... oh, shit... fuck..." I pant.

"Fucking little cunt, you feel so good... you're gonna make me cum so hard." He isn't letting up and the assault is pushing me right over. He hasn't said I can cum, but I don't have much choice. He edged me too close to death. His fingers wrap around my throat. "Cum for me," he groans. "Cum all over my cock."

I shriek and cry out, "Oh god..." My legs are shaking. My face flushes, heat pooling under my arms. My orgasm detonates around me, sharp powerful explosions, warm, wet showers as I cum. "Ahh... shit... mmm... damn..."

Jack grunts and pulls in and out a few more times as he unloads into my pussy. It's everything I've waited for all night. Everything that I need. I'm so cum-drunk that I can't even see straight. If you asked me the day of the week, even where I am, I wouldn't be able to tell you. Fuck that was amazing. My eyes are half-closed but I hear Jack chuckling to himself as he pulls out. "So fucking wet, jeezus, Helena."

He finally releases my wrists and I immediately rub them. He scoops up my limp body and carries me into the en suite. Once the shower is on, he sets my feet on the floor and brings me under the warm cascade. My body is so limp and lifeless. I'm leaning against him as his shampoo-covered fingers massage my scalp. He rinses me off tenderly. I feel warm waves inside from his caring touch. He's never worked me that hard before and he's also never been so gentle afterwards.

He wrings the water out of my hair and turns off the water. He leads me out of the shower and onto the bathmat, where he continues his care, drying me off. Once I'm dry, he sets the towel on the counter and lifts me into his strong arms. He carries me back to the bed where he lays me down carefully. He hands me a water bottle from the side table and helps me sit up to drink it. I take a few long sips before lying back down. Jack climbs into bed next to me motioning for me to curl up with him. I scoot over, resting my head on his shoulder. He pulls the blanket over us. "You did good," he says, combing his fingers through my hair.

I can't help but think about how he fucking tortured me all night, how desperately I wanted, no needed, to cum and how much pleasure he took in edging me. I look up at him through my dark eyelashes and smile sweetly. "I fucking hate you."

He snickers and pulls me closer. "Yeah, that's going around."

Nothing left to give, I close my eyes and soon drift off to sleep.

# THE FUCK

This hotel is the classiest I've ever been in —fancy chandeliers, upscale clientele, glass elevators. If it wasn't for Helena knowing the owner, I wouldn't be here. We're headed to an event in a penthouse on the 30th floor of The Club, the most exclusive hotel in downtown Seattle. I say event, but it's really a kink party. All the guests have particular tastes. My dick is already twitching in my trousers. The thought of people watching as I punish my girl makes shivers break out all over my body. It's the hottest thing I can imagine.

My hand is on the small of Helena's back as I guide us to the elevator. It's late and we're the only ones waiting. Helena already has me on edge with her red sleeveless bandage dress, paired with black stilettos. Her chocolate hued eyes stare out from under her blunt bangs as she licks her red lips. She's eyeing me like I'm prey. Unfortunately for her, the opposite is true. I have the remote to her vibrator butt plug in my pocket and I intend on driving her to the brink.

I flick it on and she immediately throws her head back with a moan. My cock is throbbing just watching her. I turn it off, giving her a reprieve, but she steps towards me. Nope. That's not happening. I decide what's next. I flick the switch to level five.

She balls her fists. "Fuck... jeezus..."

Once more I turn it off—she looks like she is about to combust. I'm not ready for that, not just yet. I eye her from across the elevator, waiting till she's ready for more. The moment that she glances over at me, I flick the vibrator to pulse.

"Unh... shit... fuck, yeah..." Helena's rubbing herself through her dress, seeking friction, and mewling like a cat in heat. Between the Ben Wa balls in her pussy and the vibrator in her ass, she's about to lose it. She moans, "Please..."

I switch off the vibrator. Now she's fucking ready. I slam my palm into the emergency stop button. In two steps I'm on her. My hands ride up her back. My voice is low, almost a whisper. "Please what?"

She squirms in my arms, pushing against my chest with her hands, as if she's trying to get away. But I know that's the last thing she wants. I lick the side of her face. Her chest is heaving against me. Her head is shaking like she's nearing delirium. "Please, Jack..."

I switch on the vibrator one more time. "Tell me..." I grip her tightly.

She licks her lips. "Fuck..."

"Fuck what, little cunt?" I grasp her lower lip with my teeth.

"Me... fuck me..." she groans, rubbing her thighs together.

That's my cue. I reach between her legs and pull out the Ben Wa balls by the string. I bring them up to my mouth, dipping them inside to clean them off —that and so I can taste her sweet ass pussy. I slide them into my jacket pocket. I shimmy her dress over her hips. She's shaking, her legs are like jelly. She's ready for me, so fucking ready. I unzip my trousers, lowering them over my hips and pulling out my rock-hard cock. I give it a few rough tugs. "This what you want?" I growl by her ear.

She swallows hard and moans a breathy, "Yes..."

Helena's the kind of person who's always in control in her life. She strives for perfection in every way. Though I've broken through some of her walls, I've never seen her unravel like this before. *Fuck.* This is going to be fun. Filled with passion, I instantly lift her slight body and I press her against the glass wall of the elevator. Her eyes sparkle with city lights as she wraps her legs around my waist. Not a moment to waste, I thrust my cock into her wet, needy pussy. She curses, then grabs my head like she's holding on for the ride. I roll my hips, dipping in and out of her. Her body tenses and she pushes her tits into my face. I slow things down—I know she's close to the edge and I'm not ready for her to cum.

"Oh, Jack..." she moans.

I nuzzle her neck. "You want something, little cunt?"

"More," she breathes, licking my earlobe.

"You asked for it." I grab her hips and plunge into her.

She's bouncing up and down on my dick, rubbing her clit against me. She grabs my neck digging her fingernails into my skin. "Oh yeah, oh fuck yeah..." she cries.

She feels so fucking good but I'm not ready to

cum yet. When I do, I'm gonna be looking at that ass. I lift her off me, setting her feet back on the floor. She looks like she's going to kill me. "Cocksucker! Asshole!" she screams as she pounds her fists on my chest and stomach.

I restrain her wrists with one hand and whisper, "You're still gonna get off. Right here." I pat my thigh.

She spits at me. "Motherfucker!"

My voice is husky with a thread of danger underneath. "Gonna need to earn it now." I lean down, looking right into her dark eyes. "We're going upstairs and you will be a good girl."

Her eyes narrow. "Never!" she hisses.

I pin her arms behind her back. "And if you behave, I might let you cum."

Her chest is heaving. "Fuck you, Jack!"

I chuckle. "You're gonna be really uncomfortable tonight." I press her against the elevator wall. "Cause all I know is I'm gonna get off. With or without you."

She swallows hard, about to say something smart. I put my hand over her mouth. "Do yourself a favor, don't say anything." She remains quiet. I brush her hair with my hand. "Good girl. Make daddy proud and I'll let you get off on my leg."

She looks up at me through her dark eyelashes as if she's about to submit. But then she lunges forward and bites my chest. "Little witch. You're gonna pay now." A wicked grin unfurls on my face and I step back. One look at Helena, then I hit the emergency stop button again. The elevator continues up to the penthouse. I tuck my shirt back into my trousers. Then, I move closer and fix her dress. When the elevator doors open, I have her wrists restrained with one hand. She's really going to regret everything she did in this elevator. It's okay though. She has the rest of the night to pay.

I step out of the elevator and into the lavish suite with Helena by my side. It's decked out with suspension bars, harnesses, riding crops, floggers, whips, canes and paddles. There are St. Andrew's crosses in use, spanking benches, saw horses—everything to have a whole lot of fun.

"Mmm, going to be good."

She wrestles against my hand but stays silent. As close to submitting as I've ever gotten her.

A slender woman who looks to be in her early 60's approaches. She holds out her hand to me. "Hello, I'm Natasha." I nod but don't take her hand. She bows her head slightly before continuing. "I'm Helena's friend." She motions to the brat by my side. The brat who is currently not speaking. Good girl.

Natasha's the epitome of class. Her blonde hair is

in a neat bun and she's wearing a black low-cut designer jacket with wide-legged slacks. So prim and put together for such a kinky event. Most people are in latex, lingerie, or naked. When I don't respond, Natasha takes the hint. "I see you are in full play mode. I won't keep you. Just let me know if you need anything."

Helena wrestles against my hand. She's pushing her hands together trying to create an opening for escape. I flash Natasha a half-smile. "Maybe direct me to the restraints? My girl doesn't know how to behave."

Natasha glances over at Helena, who looks a little deranged. I've had her on the edge, far longer than she'd have liked. "Of course. There, the door on the right." She points towards it.

I nod and head off, pulling Helena across the floor with me. We pass a couple using the St. Andrew's cross. One man is on the cross with a cock ring and a gag. The other has a cane in his hand. There's no furniture to speak of—that is except for tables and benches meant for punishment, torture, and pleasure. I weave Helena around a group watching some woman get fucked by two dudes. I'll admit it's pretty hot but I have other things on my mind. I make it to the shelves and find the perfect restraints—leather with faux fur lining and O rings. Helena needs to get rid of her aggression and the best way for her to do that is to get strung up.

I lead her to the corner of the room and let go of her. She immediately turns around to face me, staring me down. She looks like she's ready to attack. It's okay. This needs to happen. She's got to do this willingly. "Give me your wrist."

She shakes her head. "No."

"Okay, Helena. It's up to you." I glance around the room. "I guess I'll go find Natasha. She was checking me out earlier." When I turn back around Helena's holding out both of her wrists. "Good girl." I buckle her restraints onto her wrists. God, she looks good. I run my thumb across her bottom lip. "Take off the dress." She glares at me but she does it. She unzips it and slides it down her body, until it pools at her feet. As usual she isn't wearing panties or a bra, so she's only in her black heels. "Shoes too, cum slut. Won't need those where you're going." She leans down and lifts each one off. She's now standing barefoot on the wooden floor. "Give me your hands." She pauses and I wonder if we're going to have another problem, but she holds them out again. I fasten them to the suspension bar that was hanging from the ceiling.

I glance around, then see a rack with spreader bars. Perfect. I stride over and pick out the perfect one. I'm going to leave her feet on the floor this time. I fasten her ankles to the restraints. "Ready?"

She nods.

She's so quiet, it's a little unnerving. I'm used to the barrage of insults and her fighting me, tooth and nail. I grab onto the bar extending it and lock it into place. Last little treat. I pull a pair of nipple clamps out of my pocket and fasten one to each nipple. She shrieks and throws her head back. This is going to be fun.

I shrug my jacket off my shoulders and lay it across a nearby spanking bench. Staring Helena down, I roll up my sleeves. Her chest is heaving. Her legs locked open means she can't get any of the friction she is seeking. Her head falls back as I come closer. I run my nose along her jaw bone. "So you didn't want to behave." My fingers graze her breasts, her back, and her ass as I circle her body. "Now you'll wish you were a good girl earlier." I flick the nipple clamps and she jumps.

"Aah!"

I dip my hand between her thighs. Her pussy is

dripping wet. Even my dick is soaking my trousers. This is getting me so hot. "Maybe you need a little spanking," I whisper in her ear. Reaching down I grab the paddle off of the spanking bench. I run a finger down her center, then circle her again. Without further warning I smack her ass, hard.

"Fuck..." she cries as her head drops back.

"Mmm... you like that." I smack the paddle against her other ass cheek.

She shrieks. "Please..."

"Reduced to begging... tsk, tsk." I smack her ass again. It's nice and pink now. I rub both cheeks with my hands, rubbing and grabbing. I slide my hand past her ass cheeks to her pussy.

"Unh... fuck..." Helena pulls on her restraints.

I grab her hips and rub my hard cock against her ass. "Oh, what I'd do with you," I groan. I move to her front again, flicking each nipple clamp. She curses. I rub her clit forcefully, dipping my fingers inside her. Once she's all worked up, I stick my fingers into her mouth. "I'm gonna fuck the bad girl out of you now," I say as my teeth graze her ear.

She moans and twists.

I lean down and release her ankles from the spreader bar. I rub her ankles briefly before standing and sizing her up. She's beyond ready. It won't take much. Same here. Teasing her all night, drove me to the brink too. I unbutton my shirt, leaving it on. Then I unzip my pants and pull out my wet, dripping, throbbing cock. I grab onto it and push it closer to her. "You want this D."

She nods. "Yes..."

"Wrap your legs around me." I thrust in all at once.

"Jeezus, Jack..." she moans.

I grab ahold of her hips. "Hold on." I thrust into her with such power that she immediately screams out my name. Her pussy tightens around me, pulsing against my dick. Fuck. "Cum for me," I groan.

"Uh...oh... fuck..."

"That's right, give it to me," I moan. The suspension bar chains are clanging loudly, I'm afraid I'm gonna tear it out of the ceiling cause I'm hitting it so hard.

She screams and curses as she cums. I fall over the edge with her, cumming so hard in her tight pussy. "Ahh, fuck... you feel so good... shit." I groan. Helena suddenly bursts into tears, which is completely out of character. I know something's up. I pull out immediately, release her from the restraints, and she falls into my arms. "You alright?"

"Yeah... it was... fucking amazing."

I wipe the tears from her cheeks. I take off my shirt and wrap it around her shoulders, then pick her up in my arms. "Such a good fucking girl."

She nestles into my neck.

"Come on, daddy's gonna take you home."

## THE BONUS ROUND
### END OF AUGUST 2024

After a brutal workout in the gym, I head into the sauna. It's my favorite time of day cause no one's there that early. I usually have the whole place to myself. I shower in the locker room and then with a white towel wrapped around my waist, I push open the sauna door. I step over the first wooden bench and sit down on the upper level. I lean my back against the wall, breathing in the steam. It feels so good. I close my eyes and start to unwind.

The sauna door creaks open and a sweet, clean scent permeates the room. When I open my eyes, I see a gorgeous redhead with long wavy hair has joined me. I sniff the air. It's nothing I've ever smelled before. She glances over at me with a shy smile, before averting her gaze. With her towel wrapped around her, she pads across the wooden floor and sits on the opposite side of the lower bench. My dick twitches. She's intoxicating and I eye her far longer than I should.

I close my eyes again trying to go back to being calm, but now I'm distracted. All I can think about is her. Imagining what her pussy would feel like wrapped around my cock. *Fuck*. I can't relax, not with her in the room. She smells like dessert and I want to know if she tastes like it too. I'm so hard, I have to press my arm into my lap to hold my dick down. My eyes flutter open just in time to see her towel fall around her. Her round tits are on full display. Her taught body holds my attention as my eyes explore every inch of her lightly tanned skin. *Jeezus.*

She turns her head towards me and flashes me those ocean blue eyes. I groan. She smiles and gets up to lay her towel out on the bench. Her pretty pussy on display, not to be outdone by those tits. The best ones I've ever seen and I've seen a lot. She lies down on the towel, her feet towards me. One knee bent, I have a clear view of her pussy—and her narrow strip of red hair. I need to touch her. I want to devour her and make her fucking scream.

I lean into the wall and discreetly rub my cock.

Although it's clothing optional, no one has ever gotten naked while I'm in here. I know she wants me, but I'm no fool. I won't do anything until she tells me what she wants.

Her leg drops open and I see everything. Damn. My body's shaking, I want her so bad. I try not to look but it's impossible. She's grazing her fingertips lightly over her nipples. She lets out the hottest little moan and I'm done. I need to get out of here before I do something I regret. I stand up and step down to the floor just as her fingers dip into her pussy. I wait across the room. "If you want something you better say so," I say.

She glances over at me. "I want something."

"Say it."

"I-I want you to lick me," she moans.

My heart pounds in my chest. I instantly drop my towel and go to her. That scent. What is it? It's driving me insane. I kneel on the bench, spreading her thighs open with my hands. She's so fucking beautiful. That pussy. I dive between her legs with my tongue, licking up her center. She tastes so fucking sweet. That's it—the scent, *it's her*. The natural smell of her skin is intoxicating. I need more of her. I slide one of my big fingers into her, thrusting in and out as I lick her pussy and suck on her clit. She's moaning loud, playing with her nipples, squeezing her breasts. She's already so close. Her body tenses and her breathing is erratic. She fists my hair as I thrust another finger into her pussy. I feel her tighten around them, her back arching as she cums. I groan, lapping up every drop of her sweet juice. She tastes amazing.

I sit upright and admire her. Her body is voluptuous, with soft, round titties and curvy hips. I could get used to that look on her face. She's even more beautiful when she's blissed out. I swipe the back of my hand over my mouth, then get up from the bench. Her hand shoots out and grabs mine. I glance down and catch her eyeing my throbbing cock. This girl is incorrigible. "Tell me what you want."

"I want you to fuck me," she whispers with a grin.

"Oh, you want this dick? You'll have to earn it."

She sits up and licks her lips. "You mean?" she motions to my dripping cock.

I nod.

She inches over to me and timidly grabs ahold of my dick. Her touch feels like heaven. "Suck it," I groan.

Without missing a beat, she runs her rough tongue over the tip, then takes me fully into her mouth. She nearly chokes, but she recovers and goes back to sucking my cock. This little girl knows what to do with her tongue. *Fuck.* I grab the back of her head and thrust into her, fucking her throat. Tears stream down her cheeks but she doesn't stop. I'd love to explode in her mouth but I want into that pussy. Now.

I pull out of her mouth so suddenly, her eyes widen in surprise. "Bend over." She gets up and leans against the wall, sticking her ass out. Her ass is perfect. I'm gonna claim that too, but right now, I want that pussy. My body is right up on her as I rub my hard cock against her ass. "You want this?"

She nods.

"Say it."

"I want you," she moans.

I don't want to wait anymore. With my hand firmly on her lower back, I slide into her. She curses as I fill her with my big cock. "Fuck," I groan. "You're so tight."

"Unh..."

"You better hold on. I'm about to fuck the shit out of you."

She moans loud as she braces her arms against the wall. I lean back and thrust forward, pounding into her without mercy. Our bodies slap together from a combination of the steam and sweat. Her pussy is grabbing my dick, pulsating around it. I feel like I'm flying. I'm so into her. This bitch is gonna pull the cum right outta me. As I thrust, I lean into her and grab her breast. I'm lost in her.

"Fuck..." she shrieks.

"You like that?"

"Anh-huh..."

I slide my hand down her belly till my thumb is rubbing her clit. She curses and moans, pressing against my hand. It doesn't take much and she detonates around my cock. The feel of her pussy squeezing me, sends me over the edge. "Aah... fuck..." I grunt. My body jerks repeatedly as I unload into her. "Damn... ohhh..." I slump over trying to catch my breath. "That pussy is fire."

"Mmm..."

I know she probably needs to move, but I'm not ready to leave her pussy yet. It was so good that I nearly forgot we were in the sauna room at the gym. Her legs start to shake and I reluctantly pull out. I lean back so I can watch my cum dribble out of her pussy and down her legs. A wicked grin curls the corners of my mouth. I ruined her. "You alright?" I ask, helping her upright again.

She nods. Her eyes are hooded, clearly cum-drunk. That makes me smile too. I'm gonna take care of her. I lean over and grab her towel, wrapping it around her. Then I get mine and do the same. I take her hand in mine. "Come on," I say, leading her through the door. I sneak her into the men's locker room and into the showers. I find a stall in the back and close the curtain. We remove our towels and I hang them on a hook outside the stall. I turn the knob and the cool water rushes over my body. I pull her under the cascade with me. "Is that better?"

"Yeah...I got so hot in the sauna," she smiles up at me.

"Don't think it was only the steam."

Her face and neck flushes. "No, probably not."

I hand her the shampoo and she squirts some into her hand. "By the way, what's your name?" she asks, as she lathers up her long hair.

"Why? You wanna scream it when I fuck your tight little ass?"

Her eyes widen. "Oh, is that what you plan on doing to me?"

I brush her cheek with the back of my hand. "Yeah. All your pretty holes are mine."

"Are they now?" she smirks.

I grab her wrist. "Don't fucking smirk at me or I'll fuck you so hard your head will spin. Understand?"

Her gaze falls to the floor. "Yes."

"Yes, what?"

"Yes... sir."

"That's better." I smile at her. "Now, are you ready for more?"

She swallows hard. "I'm ready for you, sir. I'm yours."

"Good girl." I reach down between her legs and get my fingers wet. "Bend over and touch your toes." She folds at the waist. I kick her feet apart, then lube up her ass, dipping my thumb in. She's so tight. I'm going to need more lube. I spit into the palm of my hand and rub it over her puckered hole. It's so tight, like she's never done anal play before. "Is this your first time?" I ask.

"Yeah."

"Get up." I stand her up and turn her around so she's facing me.

"Did I do something wrong?"

I wrap my arms around her back. "No, you're perfect. I don't want your first time to be here, like this."

She flashes a smile. Her big blue eyes gaze into mine. "Okay."

"I'm gonna take you home with me."

SHE'S STANDING in the entryway, wringing her hands. She looks unsure. I pull her into me. "You've got nothing to worry about. It's all in your control."

"What is?" she asks, her long eyelashes batting.

"Everything. When we're together you decide what happens. It's all up to you."

"It doesn't seem that way. It seems like you're in charge."

I chuckle. "Yeah. Once you choose what you want and ask for it, I'm all too willing. Every pleasure will be yours." I brush the hair from her cheek. Her skin is so soft. She's the most beautiful woman I've ever seen. I could get lost in her.

Her cheeks flush. "By the way, my name is Adrianna."

"Nice name."

She gives me a look, like she's waiting for me to give her mine. "Jack."

"Well, okay, Jack." Her hand slides up my shirt, teasing open a few buttons. "Maybe we could get back to playing. I believe you owe me."

"Mmm, you're a dirty girl, aren't you?" I groan.

"Only for you," she responds, giving me a shy smile.

I take her hand, leading her upstairs and into my bedroom. "Take your clothes off and lie on the bed face down."

I leave her for a moment to grab some massage oil from the bathroom. I dim the lights and turn on Usher. Time to break in another newbie. When I return, "Dive" is playing. Her perfect round ass on display. Her arms underneath her head, like a pillow. I kneel on the edge of the bed and crawl to her.

"Before we can play, we need to stretch you. I'm gonna put this into your ass." I lean over, showing her the little butt plug.

"Okay," she says, her body tensing up.

"Just relax."

I lube it up and work it into her asshole. "How's that?"

"Good."

"Uncomfortable?"

"No. It's okay."

I straddle her hips and begin to drip oil on her back. "I'm gonna massage your back." Her back and shoulders move as she exhales audibly. With my palms flat I rub up and down her back. I roll my fingers over her shoulders and down her arms. Then up her neck and the back of her head. When my hands move down to her back, I go a little deeper. I roll my knuckles up and down her back, on either side of her spine. When I'm finished, I run my fingers through her hair, massaging her scalp. She exhales loudly. I pat her ass. "That good?"

"Mmm..."

I lightly run my fingers down her legs as I move off the bed. I unbutton my shirt and shift it off my shoulders. Then off with my belt, my pants, and boxer briefs. I grab the lube again. If I'm going to claim her ass, I want it to be good for her. The more lube, the better. "On your hands and knees," I lightly slap her ass. She complies and I open her butt cheeks with my hand. I pull out the plug, then take it to the bathroom to clean it. I bring back a wipe and clean her off. I'm gonna need to get my tongue in there for a little ass licking. I lean in and run my tongue over her puckered hole.

Her body jerks and she gasps.

"That okay?"

"Yeah, just sensitive."

"Just tell me if you need to stop or slow down."

"Okay."

Her body relaxes and I slide my rough tongue over her hole. This time she moans. While I'm licking her, I rub her clit. "Mmm... ooh..."

I sit up. "I'm gonna slide inside you now. Don't

worry, I'll be gentle. Just tell me if you want me to stop."

She nods.

"You ready?"

"Yeah."

"Wanna try that again?"

She grins. "Oh, I mean, yes, sir."

"Good girl," I say, giving her ass a quick slap. She looks so perfect. I can't wait to be inside her. I lube up my dick and her hole, then toss the lube aside. It's gonna be like a slip n' slide in there. I move closer, line up my dick with her puckered hole, then inch it in. The first bit is the hardest, she sucks air. "You okay?"

"Yeah... yes, sir."

"Don't forget to breathe." I press in further. "Ah, fuck... you feel so good." I move deeper into her virgin asshole. So good. So tight. "You're doing so well." She moans but her body is tensing up. "Rub your clit for me. I need you nice and relaxed." Her hand moves down between her legs. She begins to relax under me. "That's better... yeah just like that." I'm halfway in, but it's the best feeling I've ever had. I could stay inside her forever.

She's whining.

"Can you take more?"

She nods. "Yes, please... I need it, sir."

I slide in slowly, going deeper with every thrust.

"Fuck," she cries. "More..."

I groan. "Fuck you feel good. Almost there. You're doing so well. Take me in. Take my big dick in your ass... that's right. Oh, you're going to make me cum."

"Yes, please... cum in me," she whines.

"You close?" I ask, holding steady.

She nods. "So close. Please just cum... please, sir... I need to feel your cum inside me."

Shivers overtake my body as I hold onto her hips and thrust into her over and over again. "Oh god, I'm gonna cum."

She moans, breathing heavy. "Oh yeah, cum in me."

I pound into her a little harder. "You're so fucking tight... I'm gonna blow my load in you... here it comes... fuck..." I groan, filling her asshole with my cum. She screams out as her ass pulsates around my cock. My body jerks as the final release spurts out of me. I slump over her back. "You're mine now. All your holes," I say, trying to catch my breath.

"Yours, Jack. All yours."

After I pull out, I lie down and roll her into me. Her head rests on my shoulder. "You were amazing." I could get used to being with her. She does something to me that no one else ever has. I don't know what it is about this girl, but all I can think about are the ways I want to ruin her. It's going to be so much fucking fun.

### THE END

☞ **Your words are powerful.** If you enjoyed, *The Chronicles of Jack Marshall: Sexcapades,* please post a review and help another reader discover a new author. ***Thank you!***

IWRITESMUT.com

# ACKNOWLEDGMENTS

Thank you to the JACK MARSHALL cum sluts. You know who you are and I love you.

To the alpha and beta readers, you guys are the best, seriously. I couldn't have done this without you. I appreciate your time, your support, your critical feedback—Kat, Holly, Jackie, Brianne, Jessica, and Kara.

To my online writer friends—you make every day easier with your support and your laughter and understanding. Thank you for being there, for loving me, and for getting excited about JACK.

Special thanks to Kat for proofreading, and at the last minute too. You're my hero. I love you so much. Thank you for everything.

### *Let's connect!*
Instagram:
@cjslater.author
TikTok:
@author.cj.slater

# ABOUT THE AUTHOR

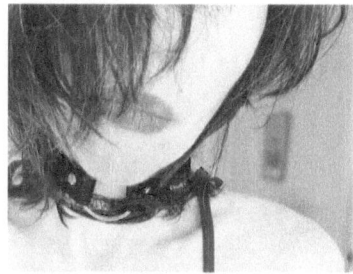

**C.J. Slater** is an indie erotic romance author who is passionate about giving her readers the full-on steamy, kinky fantasy. She has a penchant for writing bad boys whose sole purpose is to satisfy women's deepest desires, any way they can. Her latest series, *The Chronicles of Jack Marshall: Sexcapades* is about a low-talking, growly Dom daddy who likes to unleash women's inner tigress. No plot. No fillers. Everything you need and nothing you don't.

# ALSO BY C. J. SLATER

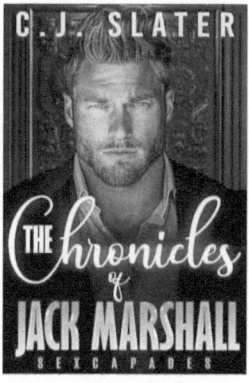

The Chronicles of Jack Marshall: Sexcapades